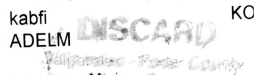

Girls of a Certain Age

STORIES

MARIA ADELMANN

Little, Brown and Company

New York Boston London

Little, Brown and Company
Hachette Book Group
1290 Avenue of the Americas, New York, NY 10104
littlebrown.com

First Edition: February 2021

Little, Brown and Company is a division of Hachette Book Group, Inc. The Little, Brown name and logo are trademarks of Hachette Book Group, Inc.

The publisher is not responsible for websites (or their content) that are not owned by the publisher.

The Hachette Speakers Bureau provides a wide range of authors for speaking events. To find out more, go to hachettespeakersbureau.com or call (866) 376-6591.

ISBN 978-0-316-45081-2
LCCN 2020937670

Printing 1, 2020

LSC-C

Printed in the United States of America

CONTENTS

Girls of a Certain Age

ONLY THE GOOD

The final time Hugh broke it off with me we drank our coffee outside the café because he wanted to smoke. He took long drags on his cigarette and then exhaled with O-ed lips. Across the black metal table I shivered, layered in a long-sleeved shirt, a sweater, my coat, and a scarf—a hand-knit green one my brother had given me the previous Christmas. Hugh and I were the only people sitting outside. Professionals in black coats and shoes hurried along the sidewalk past us, taking long strides. Each time the door to the café jangled open, I tried to make out what song was playing inside.

"This isn't good for me," said Hugh in his deep voice, sipping his coffee for a dramatic pause, "this going back to you whenever I'm a little lonely."

"All right," I said, and I stuffed my face further into the depths of my green scarf. It was no use arguing with Hugh, who was ten years older than me, a fact he hung over my head as if you earned some kind of diploma in life lessons at thirty-five.

"You're too easy," he said. "No, that came out wrong. *It's* easy. *It's*. You're always...available."

Like a bad habit, or a whore, I thought. Could be both. The door to the café opened, and I heard a snippet of "Landslide." Songs were like tarot cards. You could always find a way to see yourself.

Hugh had been my first friend in this vast and lonely city, the only person during those initial months who would listen to me lament about the price differences between Virginia and New York and also the unspecific but certainly deep-seated dreams that were slipping further and further from my grasp every time I waited on another person at the Bell in my regulation black shirt and black pants. That job, like most of my jobs—and like most of my relationships—didn't last long.

The reason I slept with Hugh in the first place was the reason I slept with anyone in the first place: because he had asked me to. I had already imagined the future I came to be sitting in, this breakup in the cold over black coffee and his cigarettes.

"Truthfully," he added, tapping out ash into a white tray, "it's your lack of self-confidence. You'll do anything anyone else wants. If you cared less what I thought, you'd have told me to fuck off long ago."

"Well, fuck off, then," I said, looking into the bottom of my empty coffee cup. I took my coffee black those days, like Hugh did, though I couldn't seem to acclimate to the bitterness. Still, I always finished mine first, probably because I was trying to get it over with as quickly as possible.

* * *

A few weeks later my publishing job (better pay than the last job, but ultimately just as unfulfilling) tried to fly me to a seminar in California, but instead I got stranded in a snowstorm during a layover in Columbus, Ohio.

That night I slept with the man at the hotel bar because he asked me to, and because he was not Hugh. First we kissed at the bar, and then much later in the hotel lobby where all of the tracked-in snow had melted into dark, wet stains on the carpet.

"You're cute," not-Hugh said, flicking my nose as he pressed his thin body up against me.

"What's your name again?" I asked.

"Um, Ben. No, no—Tom," he said, laughing.

"Good. I like Tom."

"Tom it is, then. Tom Cruise."

"Tom Cruise, I have to go to bed," I said.

"My bed?" he asked, his eyebrows suddenly bent in concern.

"Of course," I said, though I hadn't been sure which direction it was going. I took off my heels, stumbling behind him to his room, where an empty suitcase lay open on his bed. He pushed it to the floor and it landed upside down on top of some crumpled up clothes. I noticed *On the Road* on his nightstand. "A reader, huh?" I said with a smile as he pushed me gently to the bed.

"Been reading that for years," he said.

"Years?" I said, glancing at the half-inch spine.

"I don't read, really," he said. He flipped off the light. "Not fiction, anyway."

He kissed me on the neck. *On the Road* was more or less memoir, but I didn't say so.

⋆   ⋆   ⋆

I woke in the middle of the night with a dry mouth and a head-ache. Before opening my eyes, I considered all of the beds I could be in, and I felt for a moment that I was in each one: my bright-quilted childhood bed down south, Hugh's memory-foam bed in Midtown, my bed on the Lower East Side, which was actually a couch, and the bed that I was in, the one-night-only hotel bed in Columbus, Ohio. I regretted not taking advantage of the bed that I wasn't in, the one in the hotel room that I would have had all to myself.

When I finally opened my eyes, I didn't turn to look at Ben/ Tom. I looked at the glowing red alarm clock. My brother, Will, was stationed in Afghanistan, an hour outside Kabul. When he was in the U.S., he lived in a house with three bedrooms, his wife, and a cat on a military base in Montgomery, Alabama. All around the base the walls sported side-by-side clocks indicating the times in Montgomery, Kabul, and Baghdad.

I had no such set of clocks, but whenever I looked at the time, my brain calculated to account for my brother's location. Right then, my brother was in the middle of his day. He was out there blending in with the hot sand, or maybe just eating a crappy lunch. Alive, I always imagined, though the catastrophes that happened out there happened in an instant that you couldn't take back.

Through the opened blinds the yellow hotel lights illuminated a black banister topped evenly in snow. I thought about returning to my own room, but it seemed rude to wriggle around under the covers searching for clothes. I thought about getting up for water, or shifting around until I found a comfortable position, but I didn't want to be the kind of guest you wished you'd never invited in, so I just lay there thinking, my temples pounding.

I thought about how I was so frivolously in this stranger's bed, while my brother was leading such an austere and purposeful life. I had a hard time integrating this version of Will with the rambunctious older brother with whom I'd been raised, but there he was in pictures, straight-faced and uniformed, flanked by flags. Even his wife, since he'd been gone, had been collecting money for conservative charities by taking long, themed walks and knocking on doors asking for donations. They had gotten married young, as organized people often do, and decided not to have children until my brother found a safer profession. Every year since they'd been married I'd thought, *Well, they're older than I am. I'll get there.* But I keep arriving at their previous age having progressed neither in their direction nor in any particular direction whatsoever.

In less than a month, my brother would be on leave, and after going home, he would come up to New York to attend a wedding and then stay with me for a few days. I knew that he was staying mainly because my mother had written to him worried, and because my brother was dutiful in each of his roles, whether chosen or assigned.

Every time my mother called me, I answered in a hoarse voice. This was because she called early in the morning, and I was often hungover, or at the very least extremely tired. What my parents didn't understand was that, while in Virginia I might've been considered wild, compared to the rest of New York I was tame. My former coworker Zona, a tall and attractive woman, had had a threesome with two of the office boys, after which she quit in order to create handmade paper quilts out of ripped-up Harlequin romance novels. How could she afford such a pursuit? Apparently, she was living with an old man who watched her through a peephole that they both more or less pretended didn't exist. Financially, the three-way sealed the deal. How did I know this? I don't remember. Maybe it was just a nasty rumor. Her father had fucked her when she was eleven. She told me this one morning by the Keurig, the corporate coffee maker, as her little K-Cup of dark magic blend coffee tumbled into the wastebasket.

"Fucked you?" I repeated.

She shrugged as if to say, "Fucked, shmucked. Shit happens." Zona did make a lot of things up, so you never could tell with her, about any of it, but shit does happen, and it was just such an incident that could set one's life on a course in which it seemed reasonable to have a three-way for rent money.

When I returned to my desk with my own cup of dark magic blend coffee, I thought about the summer I turned eight, when a friend of my father's stayed with us after he had just been kicked out of the house where his wife and two daughters lived. I'd called him Bee because on Saturday mornings he'd take me—just me!— to the Ice Cream Shack for honey ice cream. After I'd licked off the drizzled honey and smoothed the ice-cream scoop into a beige ball, he'd say, "Honey," so I'd laugh, and then he'd ask, "Can I have a lick?" I'd offer him as much as he wanted, but he'd take only one slow lick and then hand the cone back to me, saying, "You're my girl!" I would finish the entire thing myself, sticky everywhere, while he watched with a smile.

Very late at night, he'd come into my room, closing the door behind him. "Bzzz," he'd whisper, waking me up. "Can I sit here?" he'd whisper, and he'd sit there on the corner of my bed, or sometimes lie there beside me in his boxer shorts under my bright quilt, his knees resting in the crook of my knees. I knew that this was a secret between us, a trade for the ice cream. His fingers would stroke my bare arm so gently it was as if they were hovering above me, the way it might feel if a bee were to fly a millimeter above the skin.

One hot summer afternoon, Bee was suddenly standing in the driveway beside his packed car. Before driving off, he nodded at both my parents, then shook my hand. His hand was so large that it enveloped mine completely. I ran down the driveway waving after him until he disappeared.

Many years later in New York, I was whispering to my mother on the phone under a hot, dark cocoon of covers. I had come home too drunk to pull out the couch, and all night my limbs had sunk down through the cracks between the cushions. I told my mother I'd seen a movie starring a guy who looked a little like Bee. It surprised even me when I said this, as if Bee reappeared in my memory the very moment his name came out of my mouth. "Whatever happened to Bee?" I asked. I brought my mouth to the edge of the blankets, surfacing for air, and then went back under. Finally she said, quietly, "I wish I'd said something about that. I wish I had."

But nothing had really happened with Bee, and even if something had I wouldn't talk about it around the office Keurig.

★   ★   ★

In New York, I met Hugh for lunch. Even before leaving the apartment I felt unwell. No matter what we were or weren't doing in private, meeting Hugh in public felt like meeting an enemy on a brief and unwieldy truce.

Hugh stood waiting under the blue awning of the Fourth Street Diner, almost knocking his head on the scalloped overhang. I walked toward him with what must have been a pained expression because he immediately wanted to know if I was sick.

"I'm not sure," I said. He backed away from both the diner and from me, out onto the sidewalk.

"Why did you come, then? Why didn't you call?"

"I always feel a little sick when I come to see you," I said.

"It's self-centered, to get other people sick," he said. "I pick up bugs very easily. You know that." We talked about this for a while, or he talked about it, his voice deep with authority, and eventually I just stumbled home without lunch, which I didn't want anyway, and curled up tight on my bed like a fetus.

Which, it turned out, was the problem.

I was informed of this in the bathroom at work by two little parallel lines, which appeared before me like two paths I could take. The instructions were folded over and over like the church bulletins I had transformed into fans as a child. I kneeled over them, flattening them out by zipping my finger down the middle, searching for some fine print I might have overlooked on my first reading not five minutes before. Eventually, I gave up and leaned against the yellow bathroom wall, picturing the future branching out before me in two directions and then, beyond that, in millions more. I wished Zona still worked here. She would say, "Baby, shmaby. I had a baby when I was thirteen and I threw it in the garbage."

It was unsettling that a thought such as *I will sleep with him, I guess* had the potential to become a dot that had the potential to become a baby that had the potential to become a person that had the potential to—who knows?—burn one hundred people to death in a fire, or save one hundred people from death in a fire, and that each one of those hundred people, burned or alive, could also have been born or not born, depending on a decision that their mother had made, once upon a time, while sitting on the cold linoleum floor of a bathroom at work.

Someone knocked on the door. "Busy," I shouted back. I could faintly hear a song playing in a nearby cubicle—who was it? Billy Joel? "Only the Good Die Young"? Perhaps I'd live a long life. I thought about what I had brought for lunch, or if I had remembered to bring lunch, or if somewhere along my path that morning I had decided I would eat Pop-Tarts from the vending machine. If I hadn't remembered my lunch today, would I remember my lunch tomorrow? Was there anything in the fridge for dinner? Had I flossed even once this week? If I didn't deal with these little lines, would I have to raise a baby? How would I get home today? Presumably, the same way as always: the walk to the subway, the changeover at Union Square. Sometimes it was all too much to bear. Maybe Hugh was right. Maybe at thirty-five you just started to believe it, that daily living itself was supposed to be a trial. But I didn't want to believe it, and I certainly wasn't going to raise a baby from my couch-bed on the Lower East Side.

"Just the size of the tip of a pen," the doctor said, holding his pen vertically for me to see. "So small that you can do this at home, two pills. You can be very discreet." I looked at the tip of the pen and then up at the heavens where it pointed. The doctor followed my eyes to the ceiling, which was made of that white foam board with hundreds of misshapen black dots in it. "If you're sure that's what you want," he added. The world was absolutely brimming with little dots—add one, subtract one, still brimming. "It is," I said.

"So it wasn't contagious after all," I told Hugh over the phone. "Unless you believe in viral conception." I was avoiding my roommate by phoning from the stoop of my apartment building, shivering in the cold in my pajamas and green scarf.

"Excuse me?" he said.

"I'm sorry. I just thought I should tell you. It's not yours, of course. It's all being taken care of."

"Someone else," he said flatly. My behind was as cold as a block of ice. I rested the phone between my cheek and shoulder and sat on the stoop, hugging myself tightly.

"You and I weren't together," I said, though we had never, officially, been together.

"You get yourself into these situations," he said.

"What situations?" He knew about many of the people I'd been with in New York, at least the few I'd been with in those initial months when Hugh and I had talked on the phone as friends, but none of them, I thought, had become situations. "You're the only one I'm going to tell about this."

"What about the guy? What about your roommate? Who's going to be with you when you do this?"

The guy? My roommate? "Nobody, I guess," I said. I bit my lip to stop myself from making the tearful noises that I knew were coming.

"Also," I said, and then paused, realizing what I was about to say. I bit my lip harder, hoping to achieve some poise, and when I felt the stale iron taste of blood in my mouth, I tried again. "Also," I said, "I guess I don't want to see you anymore."

There was no way I could adequately prepare for my brother's arrival. I had to take the second of the two pills the following day, on the first full day of his visit. It wasn't the kind of thing you could time conveniently. *Kill pills,* I thought, shaking the bottle so I could hear the lone pill knocking up and down, trying to escape. That second pill was the one that really did it, the ultimate Undo button. For a moment it seemed easy to get rid of something you didn't want.

My roommate, Cherry, was gone for the weekend, to this cabin in Vermont. She had brought along about five books on edible mushrooms, and I kept imagining the dramatic scene in which she would be poisoned and I would suddenly and miraculously get to live alone.

We'd never gotten much furniture. The living room doubled as my bedroom, with the couch as my bed. We used books piled high as bedside tables and shelves, topped them with knickknacks and water glasses and my red-eyed alarm clock. There was no way to make the room presentable, so I moved on to the more manageable kitchen, where I balanced my laptop on top of the fridge and played "Stairway to Heaven" on repeat while washing the dishes.

When I heard the heavy knock at the door, I was half asleep on the couch with my yellow plastic kitchen gloves still on, my hands hanging off the edge so that a puddle of water had formed on the wooden floor beneath them.

I opened the door and for the briefest moment I wondered what this uniformed man was doing here looking so stoic, but of course it was Will, straight from the wedding. He had our father's broad, sloping nose and our mother's thin, rectangular mouth.

"Someone let me in downstairs," he said. "You've got to be careful with that."

I threw out my arms for a hug, but he held out a hand to stop me.

"Not in uniform," he said.

I directed him to Cherry's room. There wasn't much floor space, so he tucked his suitcase neatly alongside Cherry's painted burgundy dresser.

"I'm sorry it's so small," I said from the doorway.

"It's like...a barrack for hipsters," he said, glancing around. The word "hipster" sounded remarkably Southern coming out of his mouth. New York had already worked the twang out of me.

He changed in the bathroom, emerging in gray sweatpants and a T-shirt. "Now?" I asked, giving him a hug. When I brushed my teeth later, his uniform was hung carefully from the hook behind the bathroom door. It was so flat and unwrinkled that it didn't seem like anyone had worn it at all.

The next morning Will was up long before I was, and when I looked at the alarm clock there was nothing I had to account for. I could hear him in the kitchen, washing and drying my dishes, clinking them quietly on top of one another and humming a little. I wondered if he was humming for his own benefit or for mine. In our childhood, no matter how mercilessly he had been torturing me not hours or minutes before, he would know when I was really upset. Sometimes he would simply retreat, but other times he would switch the game to something gentler and start humming songs in his own version of *Name That Tune*.

When I was in eighth grade, a classmate I'd known for many years was hit by a car while riding her bike. Three days later, she died. When they told us this in the morning at school, I was unable to assimilate the information. I walked around all day in quiet, silent denial.

But that night, I started crying and couldn't stop. I cried until my brother entered my room without a word, began scratching my back and humming. He hummed just one song and I didn't try to guess what it was. Hours later, my mother found us both sound asleep, my arm flung gently and haphazardly across my brother's waist. She woke us up, shaking me by the shoulder. "You have your own beds," she said in a whisper. "Use them."

★   ★   ★

I ambled into the kitchen without bothering to brush my teeth or look at my face. My brother was still in his sweats, but he looked wide-awake. He hummed around the kitchen, stacking dishes. "You don't need to do that," I said. "I'll do it later." But he kept on stacking, and before I knew it a plate of eggs was staring up at me.

"Want some?" he asked.

I didn't want anything, especially not eggs. "Sure," I said. I took a giant bite of egg, the yellow bursting in my mouth. A book about military strategy was spread upside down on the table. I could see all of the dots of the *i*'s staring up at me from the blurbs on the back cover. The egg swam around in my mouth until I finally swallowed it.

If you separated us into our different environments—me in this messy apartment, him in the desert wearing fatigues or at home with his wife—you could no longer tell that we had come from the same place, but neither could you determine when we'd diverged, what choices we had made or what choices had been made for us.

It was hard to tell when people grew up, exactly, or why. When had my brother decided to stop tying my hair to the kitchen chairs? To stop locking me in the bathroom? To stop shooting rubber bands in my face?

"What happened to your lip?" Will asked, taking my empty plate to wash.

"Anxiety," I said.

* * *

My brother and I rented a movie, the way we used to do when our parents were both out of town and he was supposed to keep an eye on me. We were never a more united front than when our parents left us to our own devices. I took the second pill before the movie while my brother was at a lamp, picking off ladybugs and putting them on the face of the building just outside the window.

I lay on the couch, and my brother took the rocking chair.

"Are you sure you want to watch a war movie?" I asked.

"Every movie is a kind of war movie," he said. "Everyone's fighting for something."

"Everyone's fighting *against* something," I corrected.

As usual, I couldn't figure out who the enemy was, but I was pretty sure that Will could, though he was tipped forward onto the front of the wooden rocker in what might have been suspense. As the bodies piled up, I wondered if a life was more or less important to a soldier than it was to someone else.

I thought for a moment about Ben/Tom, who had unknowingly embedded half of his genetic information inside my body. I wondered if it was the half that had smiled so charmingly across the bar, or if it was the half that didn't like to read. I thought of Hugh, who I hadn't heard from since our last conversation, who I had vaguely hoped would stop by, call, send an email.

Just as gunfire broke out onscreen for the third or fourth time, my stomach gave a violent lurch and then felt as if it were being tied into tight and intricate knots. I tiptoed to the bathroom around the back of the rocking chair, where Will was still leaning intently forward.

Some time later, maybe the credits were rolling, my brother's voice came through the bathroom door. "Are you okay in there? Hey, are you okay?"

Maybe I groaned a little.

When he entered, I was curled in a ball, grabbing my shins with both hands. I felt like a sponge being squeezed dry. I could feel liquid pooling around me, which I knew was blood. I wondered about that little dot, that mysterious possible future, expelled somewhere on the bathroom floor. That was what I had wanted— I didn't wish myself on anyone.

"Oh my God," said my brother. He had seen all kinds of people with blood all around them, but they had never been his sister on the bathroom floor. "Where are you hurt?" he asked, on his haunches beside me.

I wanted to reach out and touch my brother's kind, warm hand, but instead I just folded myself together tighter so that my knees felt the thump of my own heart. It seemed to me that whenever I wanted to reach out to touch another living being, I just knocked what I wanted further from my grasp, and all I would ever end up feeling was the terrible pulse of my own pumping blood.

"What's going on?" he asked.

Was this one of those things his wife had been getting donations for, to save these little bunches of cells? Behind him, I could see the starched sleeve of his pristine uniform. I couldn't look at him. "It's not important," I said to the floor. "It's just a little thing."

★   ★   ★

I lay on the pulled-out bed, facing the arm of the couch, my wet cheek on my wet pillow. Will had made the bed and he'd walked me to it slowly and wordlessly as I was hunched over in pain. Now I could hear him walking around Cherry's room—was he packing? Pacing? I pictured his thin, rectangular lips and wondered what expression they betrayed.

I don't know how long I'd been crying before I finally heard him at the doorframe. "You okay?" he asked in a near whisper. I couldn't bring myself to say yes, but I didn't want to say no, so I didn't say anything at all.

I heard him come toward me. I felt the bed shift, a hand spread out gently across my back, the fingers wide the way one might carefully palm an infant. I felt it first, through his hand, the slow, plaintive hum, so deep that it seemed to reverberate through me, seemed to enter every corner of my body the way a noise might echo through an empty church. I had never heard him hum that deeply and didn't think there was anyone else who could. I cried harder, but only because he was so kind, my brother, to lie at my side, wanting nothing more than to comfort me.

ELEGY

Age 35. With them absent now for years you find yourself standing straighter, aching less, running faster. You sleep prone. You can do the military crawl. In the park women run past with neon sports bras, tanned stomachs. Little girls skate by, halter tops almost falling off, no thought of boys.

Age 34. When you're bored you dig the point of a paper clip into your arm, sharp and sweet and scarring. Your heart has been rope-burned from moving so fast, holding on so tight. The Man is gone, replaced by a memory like a magazine cut-out tacked to your brain with sharp metal. Who broke up with whom, anyway? You had known it wouldn't last. While he sl, you used to rub little tufts of his red hair between your fers. Once you chased him with silver sewing scissors. "I need lock for myself!" you shouted. "I'll need it to go to sleep!

Age 33. The Man has bright red hair. He is prettier than you, skinnier than you, happier than you. You meet in cafés, bowling alleys, movie theaters. You meet in bedrooms, bathrooms, basements. You meet halfway. You meet all the way. You meet crying in the dark. You meet friends, you meet parents, you meet sisters. You meet everyone with red hair. You eat eggs in the mornings, white encircling yellow, circles encircling circles. You hike together to the soft, snowy tips of mountains, your faces blushing red. His hair feels like fire. When you touch him, you think your fingerprints might be burned off. When he touches you, you feel as if you could burn right to the ground.

You take the pill daily at 4 p.m., on schedule exactly, because just imagine: your children would have his fire red hair and your terrible, errored DNA.

Age 32. When The Man puts his cool hands on the slight curve of your waist, you take a deep breath, as if about to dive into dark waters. You remove your shirt swiftly, like drawing back the curtain to reveal the lie: the nearly empty length of you, navel to neck flat and white except for those two horizontal flaws— pink lines, double dashes that mark off the missing, inset like the slits of eyes on a swollen face, the skin around them tight and bumpy, squeezing in like pursed lips. He doesn't sigh, he doesn't stop, he doesn't flutter his hands against you in some symbol of acceptance, he just pushes you backward on the bed and whispers in your ear, "What do you like?"

Age 31. You meet a man in line at the grocery store. You meet another at the laundromat as you carry wet clothes to a dryer.

You meet one outside a diner in the rain, your hair soaked and stringy. You want nothing to do with them. You are wearing something plain: a high school swim team sweatshirt, a baggy tee with no logo, a black raincoat. Anything to cover what isn't there. The men look at you, and you look down at your hands, the bare, white fingers, even whiter where they clutch at the clear container of pointed, pale meringues, or a pocketed white bra, or the white paper coffee cup growing soggy from the rain and too many refills. Your fingers are toothpicky, you've always thought; a ring would fall right off of them.

Age 30. The mirror takes courage. You start high. Your irises are light gray, like the moon, like your mother's eyes. Your pupils, wide as marbles, wider than most, like your father's. Everywhere, circles encircling circles. And below your neck, the fresh absence of circles. *Frankenstein,* you think. *A monster,* you think. *No, no, no,* you think, *a marvel of modern science.* Have you dodged a bullet? There's the possibility that you never would have gotten sick at all, in which case what you've done is cut and run before even being called to battle.

Body parts and the dead seem to float around you, invisible and heavy, like phantom limbs. In your wallet, a picture that you carry like a membership card. The picture is of you and your aunt and your mother in the backyard, bright yellow leaves poised in the blue-gray air, mid-descent. You are young and pigtailed, your aunt holds you above her head, you hold a shirtless Barbie above yours. You know nothing about your future, about the fates coded inside you.

Age 29. Before the surgery, you spend days wandering through the grocery store listlessly. Is this what it's like to be a man? Seeing them everywhere, in the configuration of fruits, on poultry labels, in the curved shape of pink ribbons? They stare up at you like eyes from magazine covers and five-dollar romance novels. You get it now, that men don't really see the shirt's neck at all, but what is contained in its inverse.

You consider the jokes you could make if people didn't look at you with such pity, something about making a clean _____ of it, getting things off your _____. It's not really a joke, you guess. Really, your heart hammers in your _____, and sadness rises in your _____, and you think perhaps you've always played your cards too close to your _____.

You seem to be levitating in a white room. Blue curtains swing back and forth as if you are on a stage, an opening act. A nightstand fills with cards, a windowsill with flowers. Your mother reads the cards aloud, all of them, word for word, even the words that aren't handwritten, and then she describes the fronts to you as if you no longer have eyes either. "'Get well soon,'" she says. "And look, flowers on the front, all purple." Your father brings you books, the funnier the better. "Look at all of those cards," he marvels. "Just look at all of those flowers," he says, rubbing the petals softly between his thick fingers. In your dreams, cards and flowers float around you in circles. They have eyes that glance in all directions but yours. You look around deliriously, trying to catch an eye. "I forget the end of my sentence," you say. Someone in the room is laughing. "I forget the end...I forget it before I get to the beginning."

Age 28. The stars align, misalign, realign. Your horoscope makes claims that never come true. A comet zooms through the sky, sperm-like. Can you wish on those? Your mother waits with you in a cold, pastel pink room that's full of women wearing scarves, hats, wigs, women whose eyes are bulging from skeleton faces and blackening sockets, a room like where your mother went weekly when she was sick, while you stayed home with a friend, almost gleeful about the free rein, watching TV all evening with a bowl of ice cream the size of your head. You wait, your fingers wrapped tightly around a Styrofoam cup— the tea bag has broken, and confetti flakes surface, forming unreadable shapes. Soon you hold the results instead, pinched between the thumb and forefinger of each hand, the way you might hold a cookie's fortune. Your mother's face is as flat and white as paper.

The doctor is pale with gray hair and a starched white coat. Perhaps he works so often with the dying that he is beginning to take on their colors. "I want them gone as soon as possible," you say. He puts a hand on your shoulder, explains again that your mutated gene doesn't guarantee anything, that the surgery's just preventative, prophylactic, just-in-case. "Take time to think about it," he says. But you have thought about it. You've been thinking about it for years. You've had dreams where you were miniature and helpless, sliding down your own double helix, passing through a terrible, quiet darkness, cold and damp like a cave, but worse because nothing could live there, or even try. "Off," you say. "I understand," he says, so easily and without pity, because he knows the other possible futures, and you want to thank him for that, you want to fling him backward on the table and make sure, one last time, that what's going won't be missed.

You sleep in your green-walled childhood room. Barbies stare into space from atop your bookshelf, sitting the only ways they know how, in painful splits or with legs placed properly together. If there were brains in their heads they'd be wondering what kind of woman you've become, wondering if you've used your body to its full advantage, or if you've used it beyond its full advantage and now it's paying the price.

Age 27. You are resigned to a fate no one has confirmed to be true. You've thought about making an appointment. You begin to wear baggy shirts, your ugliest plain gray sports bras, as if you've never worn shirts with necks that V, scoop, drape, plunge.

Sometimes, late at night, you think you catch a glimpse of your aunt, of her white, gauzy nightgown, so thin and weightless it could only be made of air.

You open your mouth—it's empty and dark. Tongues arrive blindly as worms, squirming in and out of the inhospitable darkness, burrowing deep and then departing, depositing nothing, least of all love. You bring home a coworker who is not really your type, but who does what he's asked without asking why. He likes them more than you do. If you were dating, you could present them to him as a parting gift, like a severed ear.

Age 26. Your aunt's cheeks have sunken in like the skin between the ribs of the deer that summer with no rain. You sit by her side relentlessly, like one of those conservationists who won't leave a condemned tree. *Here,* you want to say, *have my puffy cheeks, my healthy cells,* but all you can do is hand her books, water, photo-graphs. All you can do is watch as she becomes smaller, becomes sweatier, begins speaking in tongues. "This picture," you say, your hands shaking. "This picture of us." You want her to see how everything is suspended, how the bright yellow leaves seem to hover in the air. Her white nightgown flutters, her arm thrusts toward you with unexpected speed, as when, in the movies, you suddenly realize a body is not yet dead. "Stop," she says, grabbing your wrist. "Just stop."

Flowers. The house fills with flowers.

Age 24. You write a get-well-soon card to your aunt. The front is filled with lilacs. All of the cards in the pharmacy are either too funny or too morose. Maybe this is your future career path—the market for non-shitty get-well cards seems largely untapped. And what about cards for those who might never get well?

Age 22. The boys are soft, warm weights. They are shots of hard liquor and the morning payback. They are carnival goldfish, shiny and forgetful, easily lost and won. They are songs performed live that make you sway, swoon, swell, that end with a chord you can't play but they can, and you can feel it vibrate and echo through you. They are vampires, werewolves, things that appeared in the night to confess, convert, cry, come. They are moonlit shadows dancing on the wall, dark and featureless, versions of the truth. In the sunlight, always, they expand and disappear.

Age 21. You got into this situation a little too quickly, a little too drunkenly. After, you pull the sheet up around your neck.

"You embarrassed?" asks the brown-eyed boy who doesn't know you well enough to know what you are, and who therefore shouldn't comment. He pulls his pants up right in front of an open window.

Your mother calls. Your aunt is not well.

Age 19. Your first is finished so fast you never manage to take your shirt off, or maybe you won't let him take your shirt off. They are too big, too pale, the space between them is too wide.

Age 17. A boy puts his hand under your shirt. You stop breathing, your teeth start to chatter, but you don't stop him. "What?" he says finally, leaning back. "You've never done this before?" You tell him you do it all the time. You tell him it's as common as eating breakfast, and as boring. You tell him you've had these stupid things since you were twelve, and you'd trade them in a second for something better, like a bike.

They often don't feel as if they are yours in the first place. A drunken man with greasy hair and a yellow face standing near you on a dark subway platform picks up a piece of trash and examines it carefully, places it back on the ground, and then comes to touch you. In the dark there, alone, you don't dare move or act human.

Age 16. Your mom has a new pixie haircut. "It shows off all of my bad features," she says again and again, feeling the edges with the palm of her hand. She seems always, that year, to be wielding a bottle of hair spray.

"What are you wearing?" says your mother. "Wifebeater," you

say. "Excuse me?" she says. "Do you realize your bright pink bra is showing right through what, in my years, we called an incredibly small *tank top*?" Your father looks you over, wide-eyed, like he's never met you before. "Uh-huh," he says. "You be careful in that."

Age 15. Everyone at your lunch table buys a pink ribbon for fifty cents from a girl with a coffee can and too many clips in her hair. The quarters clink in coolly, one by one. No one looks at you.

While your mom sleeps, you stand at her bedroom door and watch for the gentle rise and fall of her breath.

Age 14. The house is like a florist's shop, all flat surfaces over-flowing with color and a sickeningly sweet scent. Your mom puts a vase of daisies on your bedside table. She doesn't seem sick at all, but at first neither do flowers that have been cut off at the stem. The fridge fills with lasagna and chili, foiled baking dishes, plastic yogurt containers labeled with masking tape. Your father must have called everyone—family, friends, coworkers, maybe even people in the neighborhood who you have never met. The mantel is crowded with cards as it always is around birthdays, but these say "Get Well Soon" in thin, shiny cursive. Your father wanders around the house sniffing, touching petals, rubbing them some-times to nothing between his pointer finger and thumb. "Look at all of this!" he keeps announcing to no one in particular. "Like a funeral," you hear him mumble once.

In newspaper and magazine articles things grow and spread like _____ and on every map there is a bold line marking the Tropic of _____ and the horoscopes say that for the crab called _____ not everything will go as planned.

Your mom doesn't miss much work, but she looks alien, eyebrowless and bald. Her toes are always numb. Sometimes she wears an itchy wig or a blue flowered hat she's borrowed from you. When she opens her mouth to speak, you see it like a black pit in the cold earth. "You know I'm going to be okay?" she says. You nod, but you don't know anything.

Age 13. Thirteen isn't like the movies or those books for girls—you have no craving to bleed from your most private organ, you don't want to go bra shopping with your mother or, God forbid, talk about it at all, you have no need for what is growing on you; all they do is get in the way of headstands, soccer, walking home from school in the afternoon alone without getting looked at. But you don't yet think they can be bearers of anything worse.

Age 12. For over a decade there is no "them" to notice, until one day you follow some boy's unguarded gaze, and you find them there, foreign hills sprouting from your chest, appearing without your encouragement or consent, throwing you instantly into some stage of life you don't want any part of.

Age 8. A shirtless neighborhood boy pegs you with a water balloon. You try to tear the next balloon away from him so you can throw it at his shorts, but instead it breaks open, spraying you both. You always seem to make this kind of mistake, either holding on too tight or letting go too soon. "Come here," your mother yells from the window. "Not. Appropriate," she says when you're by her side. You've been running up and down the street shirtless, just like the boys. You don't see why it should be otherwise.

Age 7. Leaves fall from the trees. Your aunt lifts you high above her head, and you lift your shirtless Barbie high above yours, as if you're pretending that the Barbie is your niece or your child or the person you want to become.

Age 0. You appear from the depths soft, naked. You are imperfect in ways no one knows. You are symmetrical: fingers, toes, lips, chest. Your cheeks are pink, your big-pupiled eyes are an alarming light gray. You are suddenly and automatically loved.

−9 months. Your parents are newly married, unwrinkled, sweating, skin to skin, breast to breast. It is all determined now. No one has a say. The little Xs play their hand of cards. There: your ski jump nose. There: your muscled calves. There: your propensity for math. There: your thin, pale fingers. There, there, there.

Pets are for rich kids

I had some sea monkeys once, but they weren't real pets. I ordered them from a catalog where there was this cartoon drawing of them looking like mermaid-lizards, naked and pale as macaroni. They were standing on two flippered feet and had spines like roller coasters and crazy tails with paddles at the ends and three antennae that looked like giraffe horns.

"BOWLFUL OF HAPPINESS" said the ad in all caps.

"Bowlful of baloney," said Ma from the stove, where she was sprinkling in the orange powder for the mac 'n' cheese.

Why is Ma always right? They weren't even worth the shipping and handling. The sea monkeys were just a bunch of dumb specks, like the dots of i's that fell out of a book or like pepper sprinkled on water. I set the stupid plastic aquarium on top of the microwave in the kitchen and forgot all about it, and after a while all the water was green and kind of fuzzy and the sea monkeys were all dead. They didn't even care. That's how you know when something isn't worth being alive, if it doesn't care if it's dead.

"You're being very callous, Ashley," said my friend Willa. We were at her house eating peanut butter cookies off giant pink napkins. Her dog, Lionel, a yellow Lab that Willa yapped about all the time, was licking crumbs up from all around my toes and making me giggle. Willa's kitchen was all white and clean, like a hospital. You could probably perform surgery right there on her kitchen table, and at the end her ma would swoop in and clean up the blood with a Miracle Mop.

Willa was thin and kind of floppy. She could stick her elbow out in the wrong direction, which she called double-jointed and I called gross. She always wore fancy barrettes and tops with sequins and glitter, and I always wore T-shirts and black sneakers and my favorite pair of turquoise leggings with the hole in the knee.

We were friends for three reasons: she was in my class, she lived three blocks away, and her ma, Ms. Mary, stayed home all day to clean and make snacks. Willa lived in a two-story redbrick house that her family had all to itself, plus there was a yard in the back with a fence so you couldn't see the neighbors. Willa had about a million pets, a dog and two cats and a turtle named Captain Eric and a ton of guinea pigs that were always having babies, plus a rock graveyard that took up, like, a quarter of the yard, where her dad helped her bury all the dead ones. Ms. Mary was always wandering around the house with a lint roller wheeling up fur.

"Very *what*?" I asked.

"Callous," said Willa, licking at her fingers and then wiping them on her skirt. "Like someone who doesn't care about other people."

"They weren't *people*—that's the point," I said. "They weren't even *monkeys*. They were *dots*."

"Pets are important," said Willa. "They teach kids about responsibility." She'd collected a load of crumbs in her napkin and then dumped them all over the floor below the table. Lionel abandoned my feet to go clean up the mess.

I made my napkin into a tunnel and poured all the crumbs right into my mouth. "Let's go play in the basement," I said.

"Not yet," said Willa. First she wanted to tell me all about how she was going to be a *pescatarian,* which is a vegetarian who doesn't care about fish.

I sighed inside myself and started folding my napkin into a cootie catcher. Willa loved to say "Not yet" and then force me to listen to all of the great things she was doing for animals, like not eating them or adopting them, while I was sitting around waiting to play with her basement toys.

Willa's basement had three metal shelves full of toys, and you couldn't even get to half of them without a stepladder. The shelves were organized in rows of blue plastic bins with white rectangular labels on them that said what was inside, like LITTLEST PET SHOP, POLLY POCKET, BOARD GAMES, OUTDOOR TOYS, CRAFTS, BARBIES, and AMERICAN GIRL DOLLS. The only toy that I had that Willa didn't was Creepy Crawlers, which is like an Easy-Bake Oven for bugs.

"So say you're a *pescatarian*," I said to Willa, just to see what she'd say. "Could you eat Captain Eric?" I was opening and closing my cootie catcher with my fingers as fast as I could.

"A turtle is an *amphibian*, Ashley," Willa said, shaking her head seriously, like I'd missed some big important lesson in school. "You really need a pet," she added. "It's, like, not even right for a kid not to have one." She had little cookie crumbs speckled all around her mouth, and I pictured Ms. Mary appearing to lint-roll them off. "Also," Willa said, "I would *never* kill Captain Eric."

"You want to know about death?" I said with mystery in my voice. I snapped the cootie catcher shut.

Willa shook her head no.

"My dad was climbing Mount Everest," I said, "and he just kind of fell off."

"That's not what my mom said," said Willa.

"Who would know better: me or your mom?" I asked. I mean, he *could've* fallen off Mount Everest. That would explain why I hadn't heard from him since he left.

"I don't know," said Willa, squirming in her seat. "Then when was the funeral?"

"We couldn't find the body," I said.

Willa bit at the corner of her lip. "Let's just go play," she said.

"Cool," I said, and I hopped off the chair and led us into the basement.

A few weeks later, Willa appeared on my stoop almost toppling over. She was holding a giant cage that covered the entire upper half of her body, so she looked like a robot with a bunch of dangly limbs. The cage had one of those upside-down water bottles in it, plus a guinea pig. She plopped the cage down on the scratchy welcome mat that had been a watermelon before all the color came off.

I looked over Willa's shoulder into the street, where Ms. Mary was smiling and waving at me from her car parked along the curb. Even when something was three blocks away, Ms. Mary always drove. She drove Willa to the bus stop at the end of the street and around the neighborhood for trick-or-treating, which seemed pretty dumb to me.

"What's this?" I asked. The guinea pig had crammed itself into a corner of the cage. He was white with a few blobs of brown and black that looked like accidents with a paint brush. He was so fuzzy you couldn't see his face or legs. He reminded me of a giant wad of dust collected under the couch.

Willa said that the sea monkeys had made me a victim of false advertising, plus it was important for kids to have pets. She was happy to give me the opportunity to take care of a pet myself. She told me this with a look on her face I'd seen before, at Pioneer Girls when she won a pink calculator watch for selling the most tins of popcorn, even though her parents had just bought them all.

"Thanks," I said. There was this weird feeling in my stomach, sort of happy and ill at the same time, like when you're in the middle of eating too much cake. I wanted a pet, but suddenly I wasn't sure how committed I was to learning about responsibility.

"What are you going to name him?" Willa asked.

"Tiger," I said.

Willa didn't even crack a smile. "That's condescending," she said. "How would you feel if your parents named you, like, Dog or something?"

"I'd feel fine," I said. "Better than a name like Willa."

She looked down at the guinea pig like maybe she better take it back. "This is just *one* pet, Ashley," she said finally. "Try and keep it alive."

When Ma got home from work she saw the guinea pig and said, "Jesus Christ." Then she sighed real big and draped her blue Rite Aid vest over the back of the rocking chair and plopped down on the orange-red couch and turned on the six o'clock news so she could be up-to-date with what was happening in the world. We'd flipped the cushions because the one side was all ratty, and now they were darker than the rest of the couch, and also the arms were all sunken in like Ma's cheeks because of her missing side teeth.

Ma said I was going to return the guinea pig to Willa, but I banged all around the apartment in a rage and stomped back and forth in front of Peter Jennings, saying that it was important for kids to learn responsibility. She told me to be quiet or we'd get a call from Mr. S in the basement apartment. Ma was in a real mood ever since Dad left, but I wasn't too distraught because he had finally sent me a postcard, a picture of a milkshake stand in the middle of a desert landscape. The stand was called Desert Dessert. On the back he wrote in giant capital letters, "HAD A MILKSHAKE HERE + THOUGHT OF YOU. I SWEAR THERE WAS NOTHING ELSE FOR MILES. YOURS, DADDY." It wasn't a lot of information, but I loved mail and also milkshakes. Life at home didn't seem all that different without him—when he was around, he was always at work.

Ma looked away from the news to stare me in the eyes and say,

"I'm not lifting *one* finger to take care of it, just so you know. Not one finger."

It was a promise she kept. Tiger was a real pain. He was eating all of my money and also pooping on it. I had to clean his cage every week or else it would stink to high heaven, so I was always walking down to the pet shop on Glenmont to buy wood chips.

The pet shop was squeezed between an alcohol store and a café with no name that made the whole block smell like bacon and coffee. I tried to get Willa to walk down there with me once, but she said she wasn't allowed, which made me feel a little haughty, which is like with your nose in the air. Then again maybe Willa didn't want to go because she didn't need to, because her parents always drove her to the big pet store, because she never paid for anything herself, not the wood chips or the dog food or the little treasure boxes that popped open and closed in Captain Eric's tank.

Aleks with a *k* owned the pet store and he had a green parrot who flew around the place, and if you sneezed, the parrot would sneeze too, and Aleks would say, "Wait'll you see what it does when you fart." One time when I was in a bad mood, my dad and I walked over to the pet store and he asked Aleks if I could play with the rabbit, and Aleks let me, but that was a long time ago.

Even though Aleks would sometimes give me a 10 percent discount for being a Loyal Customer, I still started to worry I'd run out of resources, especially when I heard Ma on the phone talking about how we didn't have any money left. I heard this sometimes when I'd sneak out of my room for a midnight snack, and Ma would be sitting at the kitchen table in her thin black nightie and pink robe, twisted in the telephone cord like some spider had wound her up there and would have her for dinner later. She'd be saying stuff like "He's hardly sent a dime" and "Men are bastards" and "Men are animals" and "Men suck you dry." But later I'd scrub out the yellow tub with Comet or something and she'd give me another dollar.

I tried to make Tiger run through a maze of VHS tapes, but he just lay around on the rug like a lump. I put a trail of food pellets through the maze, but Tiger still wouldn't move, even when I poked him in the butt over and over, saying "Lazybones!" Finally I just took one of the tapes out of the maze and popped it in the VCR and forgot to put him in his cage, and later I found a bunch of poop under the couch, plus him asleep in a ball.

Even though I didn't really like Tiger, I was also worried that he'd die, which was what made him worse than the sea monkeys. I'd rush home from school to look into his cage. He was usually sleeping, curled up like a giant, dirty cotton ball on top of his own poop. He was so fluffy you couldn't tell if he was breathing, so just to make sure he was alive, I'd tilt the cage up, and Tiger would wake up in a panic and scramble down the ramp to the side that was still on the floor, and I'd feel bad for waking him even though all he ever did was sleep.

One day, I tipped the cage and Tiger didn't scramble. He just rolled all the way down the wood chips covered in his poop and hit the other end of the cage with a thud. I was mad but also relieved because now I could stop wondering if he was dead.

Since we didn't have a yard, Ma and I walked to the park with Tiger in a Key Food bag. Ma was beautiful with some meat on her bones and a little darkness under her eyes like a rainy day and a chin that was pointed always a little toward the sky despite everything. She often wore these little blue dangly earrings that matched her Rite Aid vest, and she was wearing them as we walked through the park to the edge of the woods, and they twinkled in the sun like they were expensive. We rolled Tiger up in a big, green maple leaf and Ma said, "Would you like to say a few words?" She put her hand on my shoulder as I held Tiger like a burrito.

"Tiger," I said, "you weren't that fun and you were expensive, but I'm sorry that you're dead." I *was* sorry, but it seemed like if a thing had to leave, it was better if it died—then you didn't have to wonder if it might come back. Otherwise, you're left feeling like you do when you have to return a chapter book to the library before you've finished reading it.

"Amen," said Ma. And we agreed that she would do the honors of pitching him into the woods because she had a great arm.

When Willa heard about this, she clutched her puffy hair and screamed, "You did *what?*" We were at her house and hadn't even gotten to the cookies yet.

"He was eating me out of house and home," I said.

"Did you kill him?" she said, her eyes welling up with tears so they glittered like her stupid sparkly shirt. "Did you do it on purpose?"

"Are you kidding me?" I said. "I did everything for that bastard, and how does he thank me?"

Willa stared at me hard because Tiger was dead and I'd said a swear word—which, get over it—and then Willa's dad, Mr. Tim, came in the door, whistling and carrying a big bag of dog food in his arms. "Everything all right in here?" he asked.

Willa didn't even look at him. "Seriously, Dad," she said, like it was none of his beeswax. When he left she whispered, "You're so irresponsible, you can't even keep a rodent alive. Then when he's dead, you can't even bury him right."

"What'd you want me to do, bury it in a flowerpot?" I asked.

"*It!*" Willa screamed. "*It!!!!*"

Then she stopped talking to me, and I went home without a cookie or a chance to play with her basement toys.

A few weeks later, Ma got off the phone and said, "Why don't you join the 4-H club with Willa? Ms. Mary said she'll drive you." Ma was wearing her blue earrings, but the sun wasn't out so they just looked like blue squares that I could've made out of Play-Doh.

"I hate Willa," I said.

"That's not true," said Ma.

I was pretty sure it was true, but Ma said she could use a break and it was very nice of Ms. Mary to offer, so I didn't have a choice.

Willa and I sat in the back seat in silence with our arms crossed, but first she aimed both of the AC vents in the back directly at her face, because it was her car. She was wearing new denim overalls with smiley faces bleached into them and she had a triangle of red handkerchief in her hair, like she was some sort of farm child. "What's going on, girls?" Ms. Mary kept saying, looking back into the rearview with this big concerned crease in the middle of her forehead. "Willa, why don't you tell Ashley what 4-H is like?" She had this high-pitched voice like a cartoon bird. Sometimes she sounded so friendly I wanted to smack her.

Willa didn't say anything. She just casually slipped this little egg-shaped plastic thing out of her pocket, all cool, like it was just a stick of gum or something, but I knew that it was a Tamagotchi because on the six o'clock news they'd talked about it and said it was going to be a fad. It cost twenty bucks and had this little screen where a pet lived, and you could press buttons to play with it and feed it so it would have full happiness and wouldn't die. I'd never seen one in real life, but I pretended not to be interested because I didn't want to give Willa the satisfaction. I looked out the window instead.

It was practically forever until we rolled up to this long dusty driveway, and at the end of it there was this giant white house with a porch on every side, and a big building out back like every farmhouse you ever saw in a book, bright red with white Xs on giant doors. Instead of putting the Tamagotchi back in her pocket, Willa hooked it on to a belt loop of her overalls so it just hung at her side, and I couldn't help but look at it. On the screen, there was this little outline of a creature with giant lips, and he was bouncing around with happiness.

As soon as Ms. Mary turned the car engine off, Willa made a big show of jumping out of her seat and flinging open the car door and running over to the fence where these pigs and chickens and ducks were wandering all over the place. "So addorrabble!" she said, patting some crazy-eyed bleating goat on the head. "So cuuuttte!" I followed Willa slowly, kicking my feet in the dirt.

"Who pays to feed all these things?" I asked.

"Everything's about money with you, isn't it?" Willa said. Ms. Mary told Willa to hush and I threw Willa a look like, *Even your ma doesn't like you.* There was this black, wiry-haired potbellied pig named Suzie Cakes and Ms. Mary got on one knee next to me and showed me how to feed it Cheerios, speaking very slowly to me in her high-pitched voice like I was an idiot.

Suzie Cakes started eating right out of my hand, her wet snout tickling my palm. "You know," said Ms. Mary, "you could train this piggy, and then you could show it at the fair. Remember Willa did that last year and she got a blue ribbon? She had a lot of fun."

"Is there prize money?" I asked, hoping Willa would hear, but she didn't even turn to look at me. She was pressing the buttons on her Tamagotchi again while this big fat potbellied pig named Fifi pranced around next to her, wagging its tiny tail. Fifi was a Grand Champion and could do stuff like sit and roll over and fetch things.

Ms. Mary went inside and Suzie Cakes snorted around in my hand for a while eating Cheerios, her little tail wagging around, and then I thought I should give her a nice hug, but when I reached out she made a run for it, slipping right out from under me and jetting off through the grass. For something so fat, Suzie Cakes was a really fast sprinter, and even though I was right on her tail, I couldn't quite catch up, and then she darted under the porch, and I couldn't fit in there unless I slithered on my stomach, which I was not going to do. I stood next to the porch for a minute, trying to catch my breath and compose myself, because there was an angry feeling in me, and I was thinking about how dumb it was that the things you were supposed to love were always running away or dying.

The space under the porch had a crisscross front like the top of a pie, but there was an opening at the side where I could sit on my haunches and peek through. Suzie Cakes was huddled at the back near the cement wall, basking in the shade. She didn't seem to care that I was outside in the hot sun saying nice things like, "You're very pretty, Suzie Cakes. Come on out!" I got a handful of Cheerios from the ziplock bag and shook it in her direction. "Come on, now," I said very nicely, but she just kept her head down on the ground and blinked lazily, like she didn't care about anything.

"Quit messing around under there!" I shouted. I threw the Cheerios toward her, but she just ate them off the ground wherever she could reach her snout without getting up.

I looked around. Ms. Mary was inside having iced tea with the lady who owned the farm, but Willa was nearby on the grass. She was standing still as a statue with her skinny arm stretched above her head, her fingers in an okay sign, her Tamagotchi hanging perfectly still at her waist.

At first I didn't understand what Willa was doing, but then I saw Fifi on her haunches at Willa's feet, staring up at Willa's hand, and I knew she was holding a Cheerio. Fifi's back legs were twitching like she could hardly contain herself, and her tail was clicking back and forth like one of those piano timers.

Fifi was so excited that she started vibrating and her snout started moving in and out like an accordion and her nostrils were getting bigger and smaller, bigger and smaller, and still Willa didn't drop it. I felt embarrassed for Fifi, for how much she wanted a stupid tiny thing.

Fifi's head started jerking up and down, like maybe she thought Willa's hand was moving even though it was stone-still, and I kept thinking Fifi was going to jump up on her back legs and try to get the Cheerio, even though it was impossible for her to jump that high. I was sure that Willa would drop the Cheerio now, but she just stood there, the single O held high in the air.

"Come on," I said.

"Not yet," said Willa, and my chest started burning, worse than before.

I hated Willa—I was sure of it now. I hated her stupid sparkly shirts and the dumb handkerchief in her hair and the crazy barrettes she always wore, one of them with this Noah's ark scene with all the animals going two by two. I hated her craft supplies, like glitter stickers in the shapes of letters so she always got A pluses on poster board projects even though I drew all my letters by hand in this cool 3D style. I hated her mom for driving her to the bus stop, and I hated her dad for buying the dog food, and I hated her pink calculator watch and her dumb basement toys and her stupid Tamagotchi that she got the second it was invented.

I didn't even think about what I did next. I just did it. I plunged my hand into my bag of Cheerios and started throwing handfuls at Willa, just shoving my hand in and out like a machine and throwing while walking toward her, and Fifi jumped up from sitting and snorted around in the grass with glee like it was a party, and Willa's stretched-out arm came down to cover her face, and the egg-shaped Tamagotchi swung at her waist.

"Stop it!" Willa squealed as I chucked Cheerios at her. It was like a pebble had been tossed into me, and the angry feeling was moving out in ripples through my whole body, and I really felt wild, so when I ran out of Cheerios, I started pulling up clumps of grass with the roots and damp dirt falling off and pegging them at her while she shrieked.

And for some reason, while Willa was yelling "Stop!" and rolling up into a ball in the grass and I was trying to jimmy a mass of wet dirt into her face and Ms. Mary was running out the back door of the big white house saying "What's going on?" in her high-pitched bird voice, I had this picture in my head of my dad, a picture of what he looked like one night before he left, his face moonlit, his hand smoothing my covers, his mouth saying, "People are gonna tell you that you can always make a good choice, but those are the kinds of people who have choices." And I was pretty sure which kind of person Willa was and which kind of person I was.

I had Willa down with my forearm across her chest when we caught each other's eyes for a split second. Hers were shiny with tears and they were looking at me like she didn't know who I was.

And I guess I was kind of confused too because I know you're supposed to feel bad when you do something mean like throw things at people and smash dirt in their faces, but I didn't feel bad, I felt this dark kind of happiness rising inside me, like how TV villains must feel when they cackle, and I thought maybe Willa was right about one thing, maybe I was callous after all.

MIDDLEMEN

Grace is moving in with me because my lease is being renewed and my rent has increased and she is trying to wean herself off her parents' money. Also, the windows in my apartment let in a lot of light, unlike in Grace's long, thin apartment, which has the ambiance of a tunnel.

Darren, my ex-boyfriend and Grace's coworker, is helping us make the cross-borough trek from Brooklyn to Queens. Darren and I had the sort of amicable breakup only possible when gender is the primary issue. It's not that I dislike men; it's not even that I won't date them. It's just that I more often prefer the softness of women.

I stand in the dark, empty kitchen, which smells like Lysol, and shove the three mugs we've been using into the last brown box without washing them. Grace's mug is rimmed in pink lipstick, over and over in a pattern, as if it's part of the design.

I can see down the dark hall where Darren is leaning one

shoulder against the wall. His hand is almost over his mouth, his fingers squeezing his bottom lip, like he is both thinking and trying to prevent himself from speaking. He is watching Grace, who is in the bathroom pressing down the plastic spout of a bottle of body lotion in order to lock it closed. A dollop of lotion spurts into her hand, and she rubs it onto her pink ankles and up her thin calves. She moves slowly and purposefully—she knows she is being watched.

A glint of sun coming through the bathroom window, one of the two windows in the apartment, hits her shiny legs in just such a way that light seems to be coming out of them rather than shining onto them.

Darren smiles.

I watch all of this quietly from the kitchen, off to the side, like a stagehand.

After several trips back and forth from Brooklyn to Queens, Grace and I carry the final boxes upstairs to my apartment while Darren parks the car. On the way up, we run into my downstairs neighbor, Vinny. He's unshaven, red-eyed, dressed in plaid pajama pants and a black terry cloth bathrobe covered in cat hair, getting yesterday's mail. He looks us up and down. "Now I've got two single ladies on top of me!" he says, and he laughs and laughs, his yellow teeth gleaming like kernels on a corncob. Grace beams back at him, as if he's just said something pleasant.

I am relieved when all of Grace's boxes are piled high in the spare room, now Grace's room. I have a strong urge to push

Darren out the door and lock it. Grace and I would never have to leave. We could live forever off egg rolls and pizza delivery.

The stacked boxes look like buildings in a neglected city, Grace Godzilla-size among them. "Let's hang pictures," she says brightly. She bends over a fat box, sticking her butt out, flipping through frames.

"What about your bed?" asks Darren. The mattress, which was a pain in the ass to move, leans against the wall in a gentle arch, pink sheets still sagging from it, disassembled slats of dark cherry bed frame resting behind it.

"It just drives me crazy when pictures are crooked," she says, ignoring him, pulling out a square canvas featuring some abstract version of Grace herself, painted by an ex-boyfriend.

"Here?" Grace asks, looking back at Darren and me, who are leaning side by side against the opposite wall. It is impossible, comical, to determine where a picture should hang in a room full of packed boxes. The picture is so far above her head that she has to stand on tiptoes to hold it. Her body, bronzed by the afternoon light, looks like a Degas dancer all grown up. The short bob of her blond hair is curled behind her ears and pointing, mimicking the shape of her sharp, determined chin.

"It's not straight," says Darren, indicating an adjustment with his hands.

Grace moves the picture, sloping too far now in the other direction. "Good?" she asks.

Grace and I settle into a routine. Since I work on Long Island and Grace in Manhattan, I always get home first, and since I have

48

t to terrible things like horses or politicians or

ieces of cake. Grace puts the phone on Speaker to

ands for eating. I point to myself—should I announce

?—but Grace holds a finger to her lips, indicating

.

g's end, everyone claps except me. I am busy, anyway,

ut little pieces of wax from the frosting with the tines

get the check?" her father asks.

nk you," says Grace before taking a silent bite of cake.

getting along with your roommate? What's her name

her mother.

" says Grace. "Thick as thieves."

the pictures of your new place," says her mother. "It

nice."

ough it is all the way out in Queens," says her father.

n't sure why you decided to live all the way out there,"

other.

looking quite healthy too," says her father.

eezes mid-chew. "How healthy?"

are men who like that sort of thing," says her mother.

giant, spiteful bite of cake and then begin washing the

ace switches off Speaker and finishes the conversation

m.

of Grace's parents and wonder if I'm better off with

father has been calling more frequently. Ever since

ved in, he has shifted from asking me questions about

spent all day at work printing recipes off the internet, by the time Grace gets home, the sweet smell of onion and garlic fills our little kitchen and I am bent over the stove with the seriousness of a sentry in Grace's pink cupcake apron.

When Grace gets home from work, she immediately changes, not into pajamas but into a white V-neck tee and navy sweatpants rolled at the waist. We allow ourselves the locker-room ease of dressing and undressing wherever and whenever we feel like it. We unhook our bras at the kitchen table, slipping them out through sleeves and hanging them over our chairs; we stand over the sink in our underwear, brushing our teeth; we run on our tiptoes, dripping wet, looking for lost towels. We watch each other from the corners of our eyes and pretend we are not watching each other from the corners of our eyes.

As I cook—chicken chili with beer biscuits, lemongrass coconut curry soup, spinach-artichoke mac and cheese—Grace sits at the green two-person table, which we found together at a yard sale in Flushing, picking green paint off with her fingernails, knees to her chest, bra dangling from the post of the chair, trying to work through the mystery of her failed relationships. "In this city resides an entire city unto itself of my ex-boyfriends," she laments. "You'd think they'd call once in a while." She speaks of her ex-boyfriends as if they have gone into hiding together, refugees from the terrifying land of their relationship.

We do not talk about my exes; there are very few to speak of. Even Darren we treat like an old college friend rather than my ex. When he calls, we trick him by picking up each other's cell phones—no one can tell our voices apart. "Guess!" we shout into the phone. "Guess which one I am!"

Our first night in the apartment together, Grace slipped into my double bed braless in a white tank top and bright bikini underwear. "I'll put the bed together soon," she said, curling into the blankets like a kitten and falling instantly asleep.

But even after Grace finishes distributing her things—brown boxes splayed flat, dishes piled to capacity in the cabinets, pillows taking over the couch, pictures hammered into the walls and perfectly aligned, extra furniture spilling out of her room and into the living area, which now looks like a thrift shop that sells mostly chairs—her bed still leans against the wall as if it's some aesthetic decision, just part of the decor.

Grace is an expert. How many evenings, before we even lived together, had Grace finagled herself into my bed, claiming she was too exhausted, too drunk, too cold to go home? Flip off the light, turn on the fan to blur the city sounds. There in the dark, humming, dreamlike night, Grace's small, delicate hands would creep across my tingling skin, gently trace the scoop of my waist, the broad curve of my hips. But I'd wake in the blind-sliced morning light and find her curled up so far on the other side of the bed she was almost falling out of it.

After a few months of living together, our periods sync up and we spend days crying in tandem about our lives and our bodies. Grace leaves pieces of chocolate around the house, and I sniff them out like a truffle pig. We lie on the couch head to foot using chairs as side tables, hot-water bottles resting on our stomachs, reading women's magazines, pointing out the clothes

that would fit us worst,
dead-end jobs and the mu
be living.

But the secret is, as we s
my little whirring laptop, hu
from my cheap speakers, the
shining on our faces as if w
alone in dark woods, far aw
do, sometimes then I think I'
life I am supposed to be living

For Grace's twenty-sixth birth
then slather it in vanilla butt
before dinner to be sure to fi
over for dinner. We sing "Hap
golden in the flickering birthd
of wax dripping onto the frosti
takes a deep, considered breath
us into the dark.

"Happy birthday," I whispe
about to fall, though she's sittin
seems about to say something, l
begins to trill.

"My parents," she says. She l
on the light.

Through the phone, I hear th
voices of her parents singing the s

In pictures, Grace's parents a

cocktails ne
rosebushes.

I cut us
free up her
my presenc
quiet instea

At the so
scratching
of my fork.

"Did yo
"Yes, tha
"Are you
again?" asl
"Sophie
"We go
looks very
"Even t
"We ar
says her n
"You'r
Grace
"Ther
I take
dishes. G
in her ro
I thin
mine. M
Grace m

how to do certain things in Gmail to asking me about my sex life. My mother vaguely blames my sexuality on his lack of boundaries. "No wonder you're turned off by men," she says, though clearly he hasn't had the same effect on her—she is busy in Boston with a new husband and a trio of pale, grown-up stepsons whose names all begin with *B*.

My father's main flaw is boundless, childlike curiosity. He can find out more about a stranger in ten minutes than some people know about their own siblings—I once overheard him talking to a JCPenney employee about her abortion. But he hardly goes out anymore, and he is lonely, much lonelier now that my mother has taken her half of the furniture. He mutters around our big, empty house all day like a ghost searching for evidence of his earthly existence, pointing at where things once were. "That table," he says. "Where is that table now?" "There's no coatrack anymore. What will people do with their coats? What does your mother expect me to do with their coats?" I tell him to buy a new coatrack. "I want *my* coatrack," he says. My mother doesn't have this problem. Her house is overcrowded with furniture: half of the furniture from her marriage with my father, half from the new husband's old marriage, and a selection from the sons, stacked along the walls in the basement.

I dial my father, resting the phone between my shoulder and my ear, and hang a mug that says REPUBLICAN in an ugly serif font upside down on the drying rack.

"You're living with a woman," he says, without pleasantries. I can hear his voice echoing through our old house.

"Yes," I say.

"Then you must be sleeping with her."

"Do *you* sleep with every woman you meet?" I say.

"I would if I could," he says. "How can you stand it?"

"I'm not, like, a straight-up lesbian," I say.

"Amazing," he says. "The modern world is astounding."

I suddenly notice Grace leaning casually against the doorframe, perfectly still, wearing something I've never seen before, a sleeveless, cottony A-line dress with red and white pinstripes. She looks like a pinup. The vertical lines curve gently in at her waist, the fitted bodice frames a subtle shadow of cleavage. She glides up next to me, listening in.

"What's it like to make love to a woman?" he asks. "As a woman, I mean." I look at Grace and roll my eyes, but her eyebrows are raised as if to say, "Yeah, what's it like?"

"I have to go," I say, and end the call.

"You didn't have to hang up," she says. I have told her about my father—she wants a landline so she can answer the phone and assess for herself.

I point at the REPUBLICAN mug. "I don't like this one."

"It's supposed to be ironic," she says.

"But your parents *are* Republicans," I say. "They call gay people *homosexuals*."

"At least," she says, "my parents have gotten us these dresses." She puts her hands on her hips, turns her head sideways, and shrugs a shoulder up toward her chin in a profile pose. She freezes for a moment, as if waiting for a camera to flash, and then comes back to life, pinching the skirt of the dress between her finger and thumb. "There's one for you."

She leads me through the maze of chairs to her bedroom closet, where the red-striped dress hangs, tags still attached. At its side, three more pairs of matching dresses—that makes eight new dresses in total—in other colors, all low-cut and high-hemmed.

I am a little stunned by their sudden appearance, by the stealth with which they have appeared. "When did you get these?" I ask. I touch the one that's light pink, silky and smooth as Grace's skin, on the verge of negligee.

"Here and there," she says vaguely.

The tailored seams, the fine fabric—they are obviously well-made. But even so, they look almost tawdry hanging there in duplicates.

"Am I seeing double?" Darren asks when we open the door.

Grace throws me a satisfied glance. "Guess!" she shouts. "Guess which one I am!"

For dinner, I've pulled two of our extra chairs into the kitchen, one for me to sit on and one for my plate, so that Darren and Grace have seats at the table. Grace and I sit side by side in our dresses, matching except my dress is two sizes bigger than Grace's, and on me the pinstripes look less sex symbol and more circus act. Still, we seem to work as a pair.

Grace spends the meal moving her shrimp fettuccine to different parts of her plate. She's eating her salad, leaving her bowl with a layer of walnuts, cranberries, and cheese. She has no problem draining her wineglass. Darren pours us all more as Grace flings her fork between Darren and me, asking us questions as if she's a quiz show host.

"Your first kiss?" Grace says. She points her fork at Darren and almost hits his wineglass.

"Tina. Second grade. Swing set," says Darren.

"You?" she says, pointing at me with one hand and now gripping her wineglass with the other as if it contains the elixir of life.

"Miss Scarlet. Kitchen. Candlestick," I say.

"That's not a real answer," she says, pouting.

I shrug. There's no reason not to tell the story, but I don't want anyone else to own it, especially not Grace. Grace's things have found their way into every crevice of the apartment, Grace herself has found her way nightly into my bed, and I sit wearing a Grace-prescribed dress, which is to say, I want to keep a little something for myself.

Darren reaches both of his hands across the table to squeeze ours. "You two look glorious tonight," he says earnestly, gazing at our matching outfits.

Grace smiles. She gets up to start on the dishes. "No, no," I say, getting up too. She inches close to me, so we are face-to-face. My heart races with schoolgirl giddiness. She presses her hand into the small of my back, drawing me into her, though she is looking at Darren. I follow her gaze: he is wide-eyed, slack-jawed. She kisses me slowly, showily.

"Goddamn," says Darren. I think of Grace's legs glinting with lotion in the sunlight of her empty apartment, Darren watching from the hall.

Grace inches her finger up and down, beckoning him.

We are all adults, I realize daily, realize once again. We can do anything we want.

The evening exists out of time and space. As a pair, Grace and I are magical, shining and buoyant. We are Siamese twins with a shared brain and separate tongues. We are making love with extra limbs, we are making love in a room full of mirrors, we are a shout and an echo, the answers to questions and the questions themselves. We are sharing so much it feels like a blacklistable, communist offense. My bed pitches like a raft at sea. We know that above us—above the ceiling, the roof, the gray wash of smog and clouds—there are sequiny stars, and we feel they are guiding the way.

But when I dive under the covers, I am all alone in the dark, a deep-sea explorer without compass or map to show me the route. It doesn't matter: I know it by instinct. I inch my tongue up between her legs, suck the soft, sweet oyster from its hard, gray shell. "Oh, oh, oh," I hear her say, a siren's song traveling down from the airy surface, where Darren gets to look into her shocked, pleasured eyes.

In the morning, I take two Excedrin and see Darren out, and then get back in bed and snuggle up close to still-sleeping Grace. I wiggle my fingers across Grace's stomach, but she doesn't acknowledge them. "My head," she says, and rolls away from me, to the edge of the bed.

"That was amazing," she says. She opens her eyes. "Let's do it again." For a moment I think she means us, me and her, right now, let's do it again. "His *expression*," she says. "He was so thrilled!"

The two of us? We don't do it again, not really, not yet. After Darren, Grace seems distant, distracted. She doesn't touch me in the dark. When I try to touch her, she skitters away. An exception: One night we are both drunk and there is no moon and I slip my hand in her underwear and she makes no move to acknowledge me but arches her back against the pulsing curve of my finger, and then stiffens and sleeps, all without a word.

The morning after, I wake up to her looming above me, poking her finger into my shoulder over and over, acting as if nothing ever happened. "Let's start running," she says. It's still dark. She's wearing an ensemble that's so neon it seems to glow.

"Now?" I ask.

"Obviously now," she says. "You think I'm wearing this to work?"

"This is about your parents," I say.

"Who cares?" she says, and she throws some neon spandex in my face.

This is how we end up running down Northern Boulevard each cold, dark pre-breakfast morning, yellow headlit cars whizzing by, my stomach cavernous, my eyelids heavy.

When we get home, Grace opens the fridge and stares into it, as if it's a museum painting she longs to touch.

My father calls, waking me up from a dead sleep. "What's the matter?" I ask.

"Nothing," he says. "Did I wake you? I thought you were up all the time."

"Why would you think that?"

"You're looking very good," he says matter-of-factly.

"How would you know what I look like?" I ask.

"You sent a picture," he says.

"No," I say, but when I look back at my text messages it's there, Grace and me that afternoon in our running gear.

"You know what your mother took?" he says. I can hear him pacing around the house. "All of the recipe books, plus the shelves they were stored on. I don't have one recipe from all of our years together."

"But you don't cook," I say. "At least she left the microwave."

"That's not the point at all," he says.

"Dad, it's two in the morning. What *is* the point?"

"I do have a question for you, since you have pleasured both men and women—"

"Jesus, Dad," I say. "Come on."

"Never can tell with you, kid. Sometimes you want to talk about it, and sometimes—"

"I don't ever want to talk about it," I say, and hang up the phone. But I'm not mad, not really. He's like a toddler who's drawn on the walls to test out the crayons. I wonder, sometimes, if all his questions aren't really just the same two questions appearing in different forms: *What makes a person love a person? What makes a lover leave?*

Grace rolls over in bed. "Who's that?" she asks.

"Did you send my dad a picture of us?" I ask.

"Does he like it?" And even in the dark I can see her smiling that leg-lotion smile I'm beginning to hate.

One morning when we get back from a run, I fling myself on the peeling white-painted stoop and pant loud as a dog. I raise myself up and half-heartedly lean over my leg, forcing myself to stay down for ten Mississippis.

When I look up, Grace has her leg slung over the porch railing like a ballerina at the barre, her ass facing the downstairs window where Vinny lives, the point of her chin to her knee. "Mmmm," she groans into her stretch.

A strong coffee-and-cat-litter scent enters my nostrils, and I look up to see Vinny, peeking out his door in his black bathrobe, ogling Grace's ass and shaking his head. "Sorry," he says. "She just gets more beautiful every day." Thinner is what he means. She gets thinner every day.

Grace flings her leg off the porch railing and bends herself in half, her outstretched hands flat on the porch. From this position, she looks back at Vinny and smiles. "Thank you," she says. "Thank you very much."

Upstairs, getting ready for work, Grace appears from the bathroom with a towel swirled around her head and another wrapped around her body. "Do you remember Darren's face?" she asks. She looks top-heavy. Her head seems very large, like the bright plastic ball on top of a pin.

"Yes," I say. "Astonished." She's right about Darren's face. Even a woman who likes women rarely looks at you quite that way—in awe of not just the opportunity, but of the mystery, of the distinct female otherness of your beauty.

"Like we were fucking angels sent from heaven!" she says. Despite the towels, there's a puddle at her feet, as if she's melting into the spot she's standing in. "We could do it again, you know," she says. "I have lots of ex-boyfriends."

"Sure," I say. I can't tell if she's joking. "Let's make dreams come true."

"Let's change our name to the Make-A-Wish Foundation!" she exclaims.

"Let's file as a nonprofit!" I shout.

"I'm serious, though." And she is.

It's simple to execute. We look up each man online, discuss his personality and pleasant physical features, and then Grace calls him up, announcing the plan as if he has just won Publishers Clearing House. "Are you sure?" he asks. "Is this a joke?" "Should I break up with my girlfriend?" "Am I taking advantage?"

We come in matching bras with matching mini breastbone bows. We try everything, the full spread, blindfolds and baby oil and brightly colored toys. "There are too many monkeys jumping on the bed," Grace chants as we play.

In the morning, we lie skin to skin to skin, like spoons stacked in the silverware drawer. With no courtship, there's no aftermath. The exit is peaceful and unembarrassed. There's some strange, beautiful diffusion of responsibility. Swaying home on the LIRR, Grace and I sit side by side, silent and quivering, the sun flashing behind our closed eyes, the shared secret pulsing through us as if we've escaped the scene of a crime. When we open our eyes, we see the other people on the train staring blankly ahead. *These people on the train*, we think smugly, *these people know nothing.*

"Are we ruining feminism?" I ask Grace one day. "Are we purposefully turning ourselves into objects of the male gaze?"

"Objects?" says Grace. "We are goddamn superheroes."

And sometimes, when Grace and I are jetting through New York under the guise of night or kneeling next to each other on a carpet somewhere in the metropolitan area, I agree. How did this become a symbol of submission? I feel like Grace and I are the most powerful women in the world. The men thank God, they thank the heavens, they thank the Holy Trinity and their lucky stars and women's lib and the porn industry. They'd like to thank the academy and the first girl they ever kissed and their parents for giving birth to them. They thank us, again and again. We find thank-you texts on our phones, letters in our mailbox, flowers on our doorstep. Juan, the painter, sends us a perfect pencil sketch of two women embracing. Rob mails matching silver studs wrapped in matching jewelry boxes finished with matching bows. Grace holds the silver earring up to an ear, admiring herself in the mirror. "I always worried they'd forget me," she says—who are these people who could forget Grace?—"but now they don't want me to forget them."

"Who is the man in the relationship?" my father likes to ask.

"Relationship?" I say. "No one," I say, but it's not true. There are men at every turn.

Sometimes Grace closes her eyes, her pale neck extended across a pillow, half of her mouth in a paralyzed smile, and she looks as delicate and beautiful as a swan. I sweep my hair like a feather duster across Grace's stomach. I nuzzle my face in the valley of her small breasts. I feel the bumps of bone beneath her collar, little sand ridges at low tide. Does it count when you get what you want but you have to share?

* ⋆ *

I have a rare meeting in Manhattan, so I plan a lunch with Darren and Grace. I sometimes forget what Manhattan is like in daylight, all of those black, pointy heels and women made of elbows and knees.

I find Grace asleep in her blue cubicle with her head on her desk. She's wearing a black sleeveless baby doll dress even though it's below freezing. Grace's limbs seem almost fake, as if the dress is mostly there to cover up plastic, rotating joints.

"Grace?" I say.

Grace lifts her head and looks up at me, dazed from sleep. "What are you doing here?" she asks.

"Lunch," I remind her.

"I'm not that hungry," she says.

On Grace's monitor, a Google-searched image of a beautiful woman in a white sports bra and black spandex shorts. "Look at the abs on that chick," says Grace. "You could punch her right in the stomach."

"You know," I say, "you've always looked good to me." I reach out to tuck a loose hair behind her ear, but she flinches before I get there.

"Don't," she says, her eyes darting around.

I wake up in the middle of the night, and Grace is not in bed. I think I hear her in the kitchen, and I'm relieved she might be eating. I tiptoe to the bedroom door without turning on the light, opening it a crack to listen.

"It's like a little bramble patch," I hear her say. "It's like sticking your tongue in a little wet, mossy cave." I want to turn away, but my feet feel pasted to the floor. "I guess the part that's different is the emptiness, like a ring without a finger or two puzzle pieces that just won't fit. There's no hope of ever being fulfilled." My stomach turns, a hot acid travels up my throat and into my mouth, and I swallow it back down. I don't know how I know, but I know: she is talking to my father. It takes a moment for me to realize that he probably thinks he's talking to me.

I should go out there and break some chairs. I should smash one over Grace's head. I should be mad enough to wake the neighbors. But I feel more heart-sunk than angry. My mouth tastes sour. It's the same betrayal again and again: Grace has never wanted me without wanting something else on the other side of me.

I feel my own desolation acutely, as if she has already left, as if I have already watched from the second-story window as her possessions trail out in reverse order of their arrival: the throng of chairs, the peeling table, the cherry bed, the pink-sheeted mattress, her small body. My bed, the kitchen, the closet: empty again. Equilibrium is impossible, I think. You're either bursting at the seams or desolate.

I picture my father sitting in the dark at the head of the dining room table, the phone to his ear. It's a long mahogany table with four chairs lined up on one side, part of his half of the furniture. He is looking out through the doorway into the vast, black emptiness of the foyer, the living room. He'll never get new furniture—where would it fit? The floors are already filled with sun-bleached stains, bright as crime scene tape, marking off each thing that is missing.

THE REPLACEMENTS

I watched from behind the screen door's dirty frame as Jay hauled the body up the dusty driveway toward the house, sweating and wailing as he did, his face red to match his bloody hands. The dog looked giant and heavy in Jay's thin, muscled arms. "Flower," Jay whispered, nuzzling up close to Flower's furry brow so that blood streaked Jay's nose. "And you, Leanne," he added without looking at me. "You."

"He ran into the pickup," I repeated quietly. "He ran right into me."

Jay pushed the screen door open hard with his heavy brown boot, sending it screeching and convulsing into the dented wall as I jumped out of the way. He walked to the threshold between the kitchen and family room and kneeled down like a man in prayer, placing Flower so that half of him lay on the linoleum floor and the other half on the thinly worn carpet. "Look!" Jay snarled. "Look what you did!" They lay there together like a pair of lovers, Jay's head nestled between Flower's shoulders, below his flattened head.

I slunk down into the spring-dead gray couch so Jay couldn't see me over the back. I was shaking, my heart knocking in my chest. A terrible, electric energy pulsed through me, adrenaline mixed with exhaustion, a strange sweet-and-sour sensation, like insomnia or nostalgia or a ghost-shiver on a hot day.

Jay stood up. His gray-black reflection widened and distorted in the old tube TV as he approached. The blood rushed out of my face, and I pressed my body hard into the back of the couch. In the TV I could see his wild teary eyes. He extended his tongue lizard-like to lick his dry lips.

"You never wanted him, not ever!" Jay shouted, standing in front of me now, pointing one arm violently toward Flower as the other one scratched at his neck, streaking it in pink lines. Veins jutted from his outstretched arm. His face was crazy with sweat and tears. The blood across his nose had dried into a red-brown streak. For weeks now, when he became angry, I would imagine something awful happening to him, the vein in his arm suddenly popping, the blood spurting from his body.

"Look!" he yelled, his arm pointing over and over again. "Look at him!"

I didn't move, not until I saw that look on his face, a cruel grimace, like a cartoon villain gathering energy from the atmosphere so lightning bolts could shoot out of his fingertips, and I curled over into myself automatically as I saw Jay's leg winding back...

⋆   ⋆   ⋆

"He's not the man I married," women always say, but that wasn't the problem. It was more that while I hadn't meant to end up with Jay, I hadn't meant not to either. It's just what happens when you fall in love with someone in high school, someone rugged and brooding with dark hair and grease-stained hands and parents as absent as yours, someone who stays after school to help you with your bio homework, who spends an hour perfecting your father's jerky handwriting so you can get out of having a tire-tug face-off with Haley Nowak in fourth period gym class, whose voice in your ear is a warm tickle that says things you've never heard before, not from anyone, and whose stinging slap feels like love too, in a way, warm and passionate, and for a while the balance between good and bad is weighted in your favor.

Recently, I'd found stuck under the fridge, among beer can tabs and dust bunnies, an old photo of Jay and me, a candid one from prom not a half decade before. In the picture, Jay is handsome, wearing the crown he had just been voted into and a white button-down with sleeves rolled to the elbows. He is lifting me up slightly, like a prize, my feet an inch off the ground, the fabric of my shiny red dress bright and glistening where his fingers grab around my waist. As I looked at the photo on my sweaty haunches in the kitchen, my bare feet sticky on the floor, the broom handle still shoved halfway under the fridge and the dustpan in my hand, I understood, for the first time, my own expression in the photo. My eyes are wide with shock—not that Jay had won, but that the person who had won was the same person who had chosen me.

But what had I chosen? Looking at that picture was like staring at myself from across a canyon. Back then, I thought the future expanded out around me in every direction. I thought the choice could be mine and mine again. But the ground had cracked at my feet, and it was the strangest feeling now, to look across the abyss, having arrived on some other side without ever having picked a direction at all.

Jay's steel-toe boot blew into my shin. A sharp pain echoed out through my leg like a crack spreading across ice, and I jerked my head to the ceiling in a silent howl, my leg jumping into my own cradling hands.

"Look," Jay said through gritted teeth, clawing into my forearm with his blood-dried fingers, dragging me to Flower, my aching leg dragging behind me, dead weight.

"Do you see?" he whined as we stood over him. "Do you see what you've done?"

I saw. I had already seen. I could see Flower's cracked skull through the broken skin on the top of his head, dirty white between smears of red-brown blood.

He let go of me, stepped over Flower, and stomped to the fridge. The places on my arm where his fingers had been were round and white, tiny faces staring up at me in terror. My throbbing leg felt like some separate being, a creature I was telepathically connected to and wanted to console.

Jay guzzled down the last tallboy in the fridge. My stomach growled as the sweating silver can glinted in the white-hot mid-morning light like a piece of jewelry. When he finished, he threw the can clattering into the sink and then readied his hand on the screen door's thin black handle, head bowed. He stood there for a minute and then slowly raised his head, turning it toward me snakelike on his long, pink neck, eyes narrowed into slits. I knew he was just like Flower, that he could smell fear.

He looked me up and down slowly, his face bewildered and disfigured by disgust. Then his face went flat, and he seemed too exhausted to come up with anything original. "You're getting fat as fuck anyway," he said lamely, which was true, though Jay didn't know a thing about it, and he left, the screen door hitting the frame violently and echoing behind him.

I moved toward it automatically, flipping the steel-hook latch into its eye, and then watched the light flash in and out of the new dent in the old blue pickup truck as Jay zoomed in reverse out the driveway and then shot backward into the street, crunched into forward gear, and hurtled off high speed into the horizon.

I collapsed back on the couch and inspected my shin. The skin had risen like dough into the bruised shape of a baby mouse. There was no ice in the freezer, and nothing else for that matter. The fridge was even emptier than when I'd left this morning to get the milk. I kept the door open for a minute, closing my eyes as if facing a breeze, until the fridge's hum turned into a buzz and then quieted completely.

I slammed the door. I felt hollow with hunger. I stalked the kitchen for something to eat: empty cupboards, crumbs at the bottoms of empty bags. I found a bright red can of warm Coke. The hot fizz stung as it snapped down my throat. In the heat, the green and yellow floral paper that lined the cupboards was peeling off at the corners. Maybe I was peeling off at the corners too. My stomach somersaulted and growled. Flies circled around Flower's bloody head.

The first time I saw Flower, his head was sticking out the passenger window of the blue truck, his pointy tongue swinging out behind him. He had been named Flower at the pound, and Jay thought it was funny so he never changed it. To Jay I had always said, "If it came to Flower or me, I know who you'd choose." He chose Flower when he didn't ask me to go to the pound with him, didn't ask if I wanted a dog in the first place. He chose Flower when he spent the money we didn't have on shots, name-brand food, plastic toys that would be ripped to pieces, strewn around the house, and then eaten by the vacuum cleaner that would break because of it. He chose Flower every time the dog parted his black lips into a freakish, snarling smile that revealed his sharp, bone-white teeth, teeth that first bit me on the arm one cold winter morning when I bent down to refill his water bowl.

"Part pit bull, part German shepherd," Jay had said as if I should have known better. "These dogs can smell fear. These dogs eat babies." This was what he said as the blood spread out across the paper towel I held over my arm, the bite deep and stinging. *What does fear have to do with eating babies?* I wondered, but it was a fact pair I'd heard him repeat proudly ever since, as if these were the only two facts about pit bull–German shepherd mixes, or as if Flower were his son, as if Jay had taught him these very skills.

I often tiptoed around the house hoping not to be bitten, hoping just to blend in with the walls, but then either Jay's or

Flower's eyes would meet mine suddenly, shining little spotlights surprised to find something living in the dark. I'd wait quietly, holding my breath, hoping they'd move on.

My stomach rumbled. "Okay," I said, looking down at it. "Okay."

I tested my bad leg, leaning all of my body weight into it, letting the hard-bone ache expand up into my thigh and down into my toes until I was sure I could bear to walk on it for a distance. Then I slipped on my pink plastic flip-flops and limped down the dusty driveway toward the Pancake Palace.

I was a regular at the Palace, and for that they made me feel like a queen, always smiling broadly from behind their pink and blue aprons, adding extra bacon and sausage to my plate, bringing me coffee before I even asked for it, in a beige jug with raised lines like soft-serve ice cream. Jay never joined me at the Pancake Palace because he didn't like breakfast foods. They had other kinds of foods, but I'd never mentioned it.

The sun was a white-hot fireball. My shoulders sizzled. Sweat seemed to boil out of me, dripping down my face and stinging my eyes. Along the horizon, low gray clouds taunted, but I wasn't counting on anything. It hadn't rained in weeks and the grass everywhere had grown brittle and beige, the petals of flowers wilting.

What good was summer anyway? The past spring had been deep green and mild, and every day after work I'd walk through the bright woods down to the pond a half mile or so behind the house to watch a row of baby geese stream into and out of the water. Their eyes were smooth and shiny as black pearls and when their yellow-brown feathers caught in the afternoon light, they seemed illuminated like saints in old paintings. I followed the geese around and around the pond. Once, when I got too close, the mother stretched her elegant, black neck toward me, and a thick muscle of bright pink tongue pointed out from her hard beak in a breathy hiss. I had never seen a goose's tongue before. It was fierce and prehistoric-looking, outlined in sharp sawtooth barbs. I admired her, making herself ugly to protect what she loved.

But I stopped going after that. I was afraid Flower might pick up my scent, nab one of the goslings. Jay would probably encourage him.

The sun had ticked past midday by the time I pushed open the door to the Pancake Palace, a wave of AC washing over me followed by the sweet scents of bacon and maple syrup. I was exhausted and aching. As my eyes adjusted to the dim interior lights I felt a kind of vertigo, and suddenly I was so sick with hunger I thought I might throw up.

My favorite waiter, Freddy, rushed over to greet me. "Are you okay?" he asked. "Oh my God, your leg!" He put his hand to his mouth, and then thought quickly to remove it. "What happened?"

"You just can't imagine," I said.

He led me past the rows of pink and blue vinyl booths to my regular seat in the far corner, glancing back at me frequently, as if to be sure I hadn't collapsed. The walls were hand-painted with little vignettes from fairy tales: Little Miss Muffet eating grits under the menacing glare of a spider, Hansel and Gretel standing before a house made of sausage and eggs, the dark shadow of a pointed hat in the window, their childish faces distorted with giant eyes and teeth as square as Post-it notes.

I fell into the seat, then slid on my sweat into the corner and leaned my head against the wall. Right away, Freddy brought me ice water and coffee and three pieces of sausage and a foam take-out container full of ice for my leg. I gulped the ice water down, holding the straw out of the way with my finger, and then I was into the sausage. "I'm sorry," I said. "I'm starving."

Freddy stood over me smiling. "I hoped you'd come by soon," he said. "I wanted to tell you: this is my last week. I'm moving, to New York." He said it like an apology. My heart got heavy, and I opened my menu in front of my face even though I knew what I wanted. When people from here went to New York, they came back in a week or never at all. I thought of always having Sandra B or Sandra S or Erin waiting on me.

I forced a smile. "I should've saved up for a big tip," I said. "You moving up there by yourself?"

"Just me. My retriever is staying here, with my mom."

"I bet you'll miss her," I said, though I didn't know if I meant the dog or the mom. I examined Freddy's face from behind my menu. It was cartoonishly round, pale and smooth, but with an angular nose that didn't match the rest of him. "It's the right thing, to leave her," I said. "A dog shouldn't live cooped up in a tiny apartment like that."

Pretty soon Freddy was setting plates before me: scrambled eggs, hash browns, pancakes, bacon, sausage, all of them shining with grease. The Ultra Big Breakfast. As I ate, I watched Freddy talking to Sandra—I couldn't remember which one or make out her name tag. He touched her gently on the shoulder, and I wondered if they'd been together, if she wanted him to go or stay.

I ate everything. I even poured blueberry syrup on my last piece of toast. I felt huge and full, as if I could roll back home. After a while, Freddy came over with a little tent of a check, and I knew that as soon as he put it down, the only thing left to do would be to pay and go home. Before I could think, I was grabbing Freddy's arm and talking like a woman possessed. "I can give you another kind of tip," I said, and I raised my eyebrows slightly, half to be sure he understood and half in shock at my own boldness.

I waited in the men's bathroom nervously, glancing around, trying to figure out how I should position myself after he came in. Sweat had dried into a salty grit on my skin, and the throb in my shin had shifted into a dull ache. In the mirror I could see that my shirt was getting too tight. My body looked soft and transformable, as if a few pinches here and there could turn me into another person, or maybe I already had been pinched here and there and now I was someone else.

"I asked for a smoke break," said Freddy, turning the lock on the door behind him.

"Do you smoke?" I asked.

"No," he said, not looking at me. He seemed different without his blue apron, like a real person who could exist outside the restaurant. "I cleaned in here today," he said, sliding his index finger against the rim of a sink. "Are you really sure about this?"

"We'll do it like this," I said, to make it seem like I'd done it this way a million times, but I'd only seen a hooker doing it in a movie once, something Jay was watching. I faced the mirror, pulled my shorts to my ankles, put my hands on both sides of the sink, and looked down into the dark holes in the silver drain, leaning the rest of my body out toward him.

"Do we need a—?"

"It's okay," I said.

"I don't know," he said. "I can't believe this."

I hadn't slept with anyone but Jay in a long, long time. He was shyer than Jay, I could feel that from the start, slower to get into things. When he began to move faster, I put my hands up on the mirror to brace myself, taking care to keep my stomach away from the sink edge. I watched Freddy in the mirror, his face contorted in that expression of pleasure that could be mistaken for pain. He was shiny with sweat, plastic-looking, like one of those fake babies at the women's doctor's office.

Was it only the day before that I had been touching one of those? The pale, plastic thing was just a spiral of human, curled up with its tiny arms crossed, tiny knees tucked toward its chin. It looked sad cradled there, exposed and alone in a cross section of pink plastic womb.

Freddy's thighs slapped over and over against mine, and he began to groan. It dawned on me then, what I was doing. I wanted to replace the small, growing piece of Jay inside me with a piece of Freddy, or with anyone else, it didn't matter who. I was wishing for the impossible, for an undoing, for a gap in time and logic.

I looked into the mirror, directly into my own eyes. My pupils were dark as the holes in the drain. "I'm coming," whispered Freddy, but it wasn't the kind of coming that could save me from anything. I had thought being a woman was exactly this easy, as if all you had to do was stand still and blend in, but it wasn't true. "He's not the man I married," women say, but maybe it was the other way around.

I understood now how much Jay had loved Flower—it was a violent, overwhelming, barbed-tongue love. But I loved something more.

I pictured Flower, how he'd run toward the truck, his lips curled, his teeth sharp and shining, so bright that I believed I could see my future reflected in them, but it was just the relentless glow of the burning summer sun. I put my hand to my belly. I angled the truck just so.

NONE OF THESE WILL BRING DISASTER

WORK

I often come into work with sunglasses on, having taken the bus. I take the bus when I am still drunk in the morning. I know that my coworkers know why I have taken the bus.

The people at work used to gossip about everything. Once I overheard someone in merchandising whisper, "God, I think I can see her butt cheek," as I walked by in a skirt of apparently questionable length. I doubt this was true, but I've worn bike shorts under my skirts ever since.

Nowadays, I could stumble off the bus with sunglasses, a cane, and a Seeing Eye dog, and I don't think anyone would notice. The gossip has turned from individuals to the company as a whole. The *Wall Street Journal* says we're going bankrupt, and the people at the top are nervous. We've had two massive rounds of layoffs. Human resources is nearly extinct. The room on the second floor where they once worked looks like Pompeii.

After a few days of mourning, we pillaged the area for the best monitors and mice. In a drawer, I found a set of nice pens and an empty journal with cats all over it, plus two dollars in quarters.

HOME

Why did my roommates leave? I can't help but think that if I had done better, they might have stayed. Rachel and I have been friends since the beginning of college, and I like her boyfriend Ozzie too. I am easy to live with. I am quiet. Once Rachel called my cell to ask where I'd been all day. "Here," I answered from the desk in my room.

Then again, there are things I could have done better. I have a coffee machine with a reusable filter. Each morning, I would dump the previous day's grounds in the garbage, then rinse the filter in the sink to wash out whatever remained. Rachel once yelled at me for the way the grounds stuck in the sink for days, mostly in the bottoms of unwashed dishes.

I tried to tap the grounds hard into the garbage can so I wouldn't have to rinse the filter in the sink, but I was afraid Rachel would be annoyed by the noise. So, each morning for a year, I spooned the grounds into the garbage can, then scraped the dregs out with a paper towel and carefully washed the spoon.

LIVING ALONE, PLUSES

Once again I rinse the grounds right into the sink. I save time, and I save money on paper towels.

WORK

Today I wake up too early, before the alarm, and sit in the shower in a daze. Trying to remember the evening is like collecting beads from a broken necklace. I make coffee (I have increased from four cups to six, then two more when I get to work). I get dressed in slow motion, put on my sunglasses, check the calendar to be sure I have no early meetings. I curl up in a ball on the bench at the bus stop. I find two ibuprofen in my purse, build up spit in my mouth, and swallow them.

The way to my cubicle feels extra long today. I have to walk this way so I don't pass IT—I am trying to avoid having feelings for people I am not supposed to have feelings for.

"You're a crazy girl," says my friend Jeffrey when I finally slump into my chair. Jeffrey begins telling me about the end of the night, assuming I've forgotten, but he abandons his story mid-sentence when he hears there are doughnuts in the kitchen.

The style guide I'm working on is wonky. I know I will be here until midnight sorting it out. We lost half the merchants in the last firing. There's a problem with the khakis. They come in one shade of tan, but the same shade has four different names: beige, sand, tawny, coffee. I rub my fingers in my hair, trying to figure out what to do about this, when something *plip-plops* from my hair onto my desk. I search for what fell and find a minuscule, amber grain: Sugar in the Raw.

Where did this come from? And how did it get in my hair? What else is in my hair? What did I do last night that resulted in sugar being in my hair? I wish Jeffrey had finished his story. I rub my fingers in my hair while thinking about this, and two more sugar crystals fall onto the desk.

CORRECTION

I may have made myself seem more promiscuous than is accurate, although there have been a handful of questionable acquaintance-ships with coworkers, all of which began with me drunk and ended several weeks or months later with me in tears. Now that I live alone, I can cry loudly and wildly and walk around the apartment with my face puffed red.

I tell the guys that I understand. It seems unfair of me to handle it any other way. I give them reasons that they cannot come up with themselves. "You are still emotionally tied up in your previous relationship," I say. "We're coworkers, after all," I say.

Sometimes they will take me out to dinner after. It is a terrible thing to do. They leave me with good memories. I think of them as kind, upstanding men.

Rachel thinks otherwise. "He's a real jerk," she'll say through the phone from her new apartment. "He took you to dinner out of guilt. He wants to be sure there aren't any scenes to handle, that everything at work continues to run smoothly."

"But he paid," I say.

"Why do you let people walk all over you? And where did you get the crazy idea that everyone is *nice*?"

JEFFREY

We talk frequently in the employee kitchen and sometimes visit each other in our cubicles. He's from R & D—research and design, not IT. According to Rachel, I have to stay away from the men in IT: "Good at logistics, bad at feelings," she tells me. "They smell low self-esteem like dogs smell fear, and then they use it to their advantage. And don't tell me how they don't mean to do it. It doesn't matter what they *mean* to do. All that matters is what they *do* do."

Jeffrey is the kind of person who glows on a resume or when he's in the center of a room. I am always surprised by our friendship, as if at any moment he'll realize that we're nothing alike.

He is tall and thin, with jet-black hair, brown eyes, and a boyish face—cheeks dotted with freckles, two well-placed dimples. At happy hour, everyone gathers around him as he tells long, funny stories, his hands flying through the air. He drinks and drinks and never blacks out, which I find admirable and a little disconcerting. He's very competitive at work—he will not throw you under the bus unless you belong under the bus, but if you belong there, that is where he will throw you.

LIVING ALONE, MINUSES

It is lonely, even if you work fifty-hour weeks. What I want, desperately, is for someone to sit next to me for a moment and hold my hand and say one kind thing I didn't know was true.

WORK

We know what is coming. We wait in our cubicles like scared animals. We play a lot of Minesweeper and solitaire. No one cares anymore about the problems that just last week were important enough to require sixteen-hour workdays, like identical tan khakis with four different names. We have no idea what we will do when we are released into the wild. We will probably play a lot of Minesweeper and solitaire.

LAID OFF

"I understand," I tell my boss, patting him on the shoulder. "There was nothing you could do, and it's just a job anyway." We hand in monitors, telephones, hard drives, things we had forgotten didn't belong to us. We pack the rest—photographs, calendars, snacks. I have spent so much time here, I feel as if I'm moving out of a home, but I remind myself that I've moved out of homes before, and it's worse than this.

There are twenty of us standing in a circle in the parking lot, holding the evidence of our employment in cardboard boxes and plastic grocery bags. We look like ex-lovers cast out from apartments that were never ours in the first place. We hug and cry and say goodbye and shift our boxes. Jeffrey stands with a giant computer monitor at his feet—he has gotten it through security by employing his hearty, boyish smile.

Out here, his smile fades. "We didn't lose our jobs," says Jeffrey, but he doesn't look up to engage the audience, he just kicks at a stone that *plink-plonks* down the yellow line of an empty parking space, "they lost us."

"The company didn't just lose us," I add, "the company lost everything." Everyone stares at me, annoyed, as if I don't comprehend what's happening.

Besides, it isn't even true—the company hasn't quite lost everything, not yet: IT is still employed to close things down. This includes Mazdak and Dan, two men I personally know can tie up loose ends.

UNEMPLOYMENT, DAY ONE

As a kind of anti-memorial to corporate life, I do not get dressed, nor do I get out of bed for the first half of the day. During the second half of the day, I check my email, file for unemployment, make a dental appointment for a date before the insurance runs out, do the math on my finances. It turns out I can live for a while like this, alone in my room, never getting dressed.

DAY THREE

I have now seen this season's entire roster of Academy Award–nominated films. I have started and finished my final twelve-pack.

DAY FOUR

I watch a PBS documentary about Napoleon. My heart breaks for him when he gets exiled to Elba. It breaks a second time, and more thoroughly, when he gets exiled to Saint Helena.

DAY SIX

All of this free time, and the sink is still crowded with dishes. I find myself spooning coffee grounds into the garbage can without even noticing I am doing it. I have not seen or heard from a single person, except for the automated machine at the unemployment office, in six days. What have I been doing? I faintly recall a stream of movies and spaghetti. I am hunkered down, saving money like in my college days, but with much less to do.

DAY EIGHT

I call Rachel, but she doesn't answer. I call Ozzie. I call Dan, Mazdak. I suppose it is a weekday. I call Jeffrey. He answers. He has been playing computer games on his new monitor. He has purchased a beanbag chair that is almost as large as his bed. He has been drinking two blueberry slushies per day. I thought he'd be regulating his spending, but he seems unconcerned with both finances and future employment. His unconcern makes me realize that I have not spent much time looking for a job.

In between Minesweeper and solitaire, I troll the internet for employment opportunities. Opportunities? There is nothing I want to do, but I will need money again one day. I regurgitate my resume on several job-search websites, which then send me emails with all kinds of useless job-hunting tips like "Follow your passion" and "Polish your shoes." Still, it makes me feel good to get emails. I wish they spaced them out more over the day, so my inbox would never read zero.

DAY TEN, MORNING

Today I wake to the alarm. I have a Pavlovian reaction of intense hatred, and then I remember that I do not have to go to work. I dress in the kinds of clothes people wear when they leave the house, and then I go to the dentist. The dental assistant is so friendly. The dentist himself is friendly. His teeth are white. I think of the shades of white his teeth might be called if they were pants: snow, milk, ivory, ghost. I like the soft feel of his gloved finger on my gums. He fills two cavities—it is nice to have a person so close to my mouth, even if he is holding a drill.

DAY TEN, AFTERNOON

My head hurts, and my jaw is tired, as if I have been chewing bagels and gum for days on end. My left cheek becomes fat, like a squirrel's packed with nuts. I can't eat spaghetti, so I buy yogurt at the corner deli and try to eat it without moving my mouth.

DAY TWELVE

Jeffrey comes over out of sheer boredom. His lips are stained blue.

"Maybe you should eat something else?" I suggest.

"Nah," he says. "I don't like to cook." He sits in my computer chair and spins around. "My mom's pissed," he tells me.

"What happened?"

"She doesn't want to be paying my bills again," he says, as if your mom paying your bills were the unfortunate but inevitable result of unemployment. He could be any of the people I went to college with. He could be none of the people I grew up with. He could be sixteen with those immature expectations, with that face, that dimpled smile.

It occurs to me how much I remember about the past twelve days. I have not been going to happy hour. I have not been blackout drunk. I have not been getting laid.

NEVER MIND

Sometimes bars actually deter me from drinking—they're so expensive—but this evening is more or less sponsored by Jeffrey's mom, so it's not even ten before we're stumbling back to my place, Jeffrey saying, "You need to go to bed. You need to stop drinking. You can knock them back. Even if you were a guy it would be impressive." But he's slurring his words, and I'm suspicious of how he never blacks out. He is either a sneak, or part alien, or a freak, or lucky, or he might actually know his limits.

When we get back to my place, I say that I need to eat something.

"I thought you couldn't? Your tooth?"

"Nothing hurts when you're drunk. Not until the morning, anyway," I say, and pour myself a bowl of cereal that tastes better than Thanksgiving dinner.

Jeffrey helps me into bed and then sits beside me, his hand on my arm. "It was really fun hanging out with you tonight," he says. He looks at his watch even though there is a giant clock right next to my bed. "God, I have to take the train back home, I guess."

I don't like how impressed guys are with themselves when their lines work, as if girls are idiots, as if we don't know what's going on.

LAID

The sun slants through the blinds. My leg is covered in thin, bright strips of light so that it looks as if it's been cut into slices. My head hurts a little, but it's hard to tell how much of that is hangover and how much is tooth. My teeth feel as if they take up my entire head. Jeffrey brushes his hand over my waist softly, and a moment later he is up, dressing, and I know exactly how this will go. "Coffee?" I ask anyway, just in case. "You sleep," he whispers.

He is already far away, the way they are afterward when they're afraid you'll want too much. It is as if his hand brushed my waist months ago. It is possible that he will never touch me again.

Girls own the evening, but mornings like these make you

question what happened at night, make you think it might have been a dream, make you wonder if you were ever really given anything in the first place.

MORE DAYS

I never thought that I'd be the kind of person who spends days on end in bed, but then again, I used to think I wouldn't be the kind of person who got drunk on weekday evenings. As with most things I never thought I would be or do, staying in bed turns out to be very easy. The key is to position the essentials about you in a convenient way. I have my electronics: computer, cell phone. I need the computer to log on to the New York State unemployment website. I have to fill out a little form that says I am looking for work, and then they put money into my account.

I have provisions too: water, walnuts. The walnuts are not ideal because my tooth still hurts and I can eat them only by sucking on them. On the plus side, they don't really need to be refrigerated. I would go to the dentist (a different one), but like everything else, the insurance is gone.

In the middle of my second day in bed I make a mistake. The heat is haphazardly controlled by the landlord, and my window is not close to my bed, so when I get too hot, I throw off my sweater, and it lands dangerously far from the bed. Later, when it gets cold again, I crawl out onto the floor on my hands, with my thighs still on the bed, stretching as far as I can. My mission is a success, but my arms are tired, and I am glad to inch my way back into bed without ever having put my feet on the ground.

JEFFREY

He doesn't call.

JOBS, PEOPLE, CITIES

Nothing is ever really yours. I just want something to stick around long enough for me to leave it first.

EVENTUALLY

I have to get out of bed to go to a mandatory session at the unemployment office. I wake up several hours early. It turns out that getting ready to reenter the world does, indeed, take several hours. I try to eat instant oatmeal, but I can't bite the raisins and I have to spit them out as I go. I start the coffee maker but forget the grounds and end up drinking part of a mug of hot beige water. I get dressed in one of my work outfits, then put on makeup, but it does not hide the size of my cheek. I tell myself that I could just be one of those people with unfortunate facial asymmetry, but how is that better than having a swollen cheek?

THE UNEMPLOYMENT OFFICE

In a matter of days I have forgotten all about people, and it is good to see them again, though I am overdressed. The man to my left is wearing jeans that seem ripped from actual wear and tear. He smiles at me, and I see a black gap on the left side of his mouth where a tooth used to be. I put my fingers to my cheek.

The guy to my right is good-looking, probably around my age. "Hi," he says when he notices I'm looking.

I take my fingers off my cheek. "Hi," I say.

The man leading the meeting is small and gray-haired and hunchbacked. He looks as if he has been caged for a long time. "One place to look for work, during times like these," he says (he says "times like these" a lot), "is a place like this. An unemployment office. That's how I got this job, what, over a decade ago? During the last major economic downturn."

OPPORTUNITY

There is a bulletin board outside the unemployment office that catches my eye. What I see first is a hot pink piece of paper that says GUY PROBLEMS? MADAME CAROLINA CAN HELP. The paper claims that Madame Carolina has "the blood of fortune-tellers running through her veins." I imagine an earthy bandana tied around her head and large hoops hanging from her ears. In front of her is a crystal ball filled with pink clouds, but Madame Carolina doesn't need it to tell me my problems or what I need to do. She points her long pink fingers at me and says that if I'm going to be so sensitive, I have to stop sleeping with guys who have only short-term interest in me. I want to tell her that sometimes you don't know, that sometimes it's better than having nobody at all.

My eyes wander to a plain white sheet with pull strips, of which only three remain. The paper says,

Earn Up to $250
Free Dental Exam
Heavy Smokers Needed Now!
Finally Quit Smoking
New Clinical Trial

I once read an article about a man who, during college, earned money by donating blood plasma and sperm. I rip off a tab.

RESEARCH

Believe it or not, I have never smoked anything. Somehow I missed the window for trying it for the first time, and after that I felt too old to accept a cigarette or a joint without knowing what to do with it. I google things like "What does it mean to be a heavy smoker?" and "Can the dentist tell if you smoke?" To the latter, sometimes. To the former, I get no concrete numbers, in packs or cigarettes, but instead a lot of websites explaining chain-smoking. I haven't put much thought into it, but I've always vaguely assumed that this meant people stood in a circle passing a cigarette around, one to the next, the way people pass a joint, but all it means is that as soon as you finish one cigarette you begin the next, sometimes lighting the latter with the former. I tack the phone number to the bulletin board above the desk that I never use because I use my computer in my bed.

JEFFREY

Finally, I call Jeffrey. I have been more or less following him online, but he hasn't updated anything in almost a day. Last I read, he was still playing computer games.

"Hello, friend," he answers when I call.

"What are you up to?" I ask. "I haven't been out much recently."

"I haven't slept in a day," he says. I wait for an explanation, but he's silent.

"Why's that?"

"I've been playing Monopoly for twelve hours straight. Can't stop until I finish the game."

"Oh."

"I'll talk to you later," he says, and hangs up. I always wished I were the kind of person who could hang up first, but I also don't want to be the kind of person who hangs up first on purpose, as if it were some kind of power play.

RACHEL

I call Rachel. "You sound sad," she says. "Come to California. It's sunny here." I remind her that I am unemployed, and that New York is far away.

When Ozzie comes home, she has to go.

MAZDAK

I call Mazdak. "Yo," he says. Sometimes I think Mazdak pretends that those three months never happened between us. These days, when I am around him, I think he pretends that I'm not even female. "We're still playing Monopoly," he says.

"You're playing Monopoly with Jeffrey?" I ask.

"Yeah," he says.

"Did you get laid off too?"

"Everybody's gone. Didn't you hear?"

"We should all go out sometime, like an unemployment happy hour, you know? With the people who used to go."

"Sure, sure," says Mazdak. "Tell me when it is."

"Well, I have to go," I say quickly.

But hanging up first offers no clear satisfaction.

CARA

There is no one left to call but my mother, so I call CARA, the Cigarette Addiction Research Association, concerning the clinical trial, and they tell me they'll call back for a pre-screening interview. This makes me feel irrationally sad. I had imagined a receptionist dropping her current task and shouting "We've got one!" to a laboratory full of researchers in white coats.

I wait around, pass time by refreshing my email, but with each refresh I feel a little emptier, and I end up reading through my spam and deleting it piece by piece.

The lady who finally calls back has a voice so husky that for a moment I think she's a man. My plan is to sound sane yet addicted to cigarettes. When she asks, I tell her that I smoke "nearly a pack a day."

"More specific?"

"Four to a pack a day, probably," I say.

"That's quite a range."

"It's more like halfway between four and a pack," I say.

"All right," she says after a pause. "Can you come in for a dental and physical next week?"

Out of habit, I check my calendar. It's as empty as a snow day.

RESEARCH

I am nervous about pretending to be a smoker. Online, I read message boards and how-tos that seem to be written by people much younger than myself. One page explains smoking in seventeen steps, plus twelve tips and thirteen warnings. I feel like I'm reading instructions on how to fold an origami crane. A long, heated debate on a message board does not reach consensus on whether the position and rotation of the arm while smoking is gendered. "It is more feminine," reports one user, "to move your arm away from your face and hold your cigarette out to the side with your arm in a V." Apparently, "smacking the pack" is not just some kind of tic among smokers. Also, there are twenty cigarettes in a pack!

The people at the deli know me well. They have been eyeing my purchases: broth, soup, yogurt, juice. "You on a diet?" they ask, though I explain that it's a problem with my tooth. This time, when I buy two packs of cigarettes, the manager shouts, "You are trying to lose weight!," as if he has just found me out.

On my stoop, I smack my pack, take a cigarette between my lips, and light it with a restaurant match. I inhale, cough, and try again. I do this several times, until I feel dizzy and kind of nauseous. I notice a woman sitting on a stoop across the street. She is looking at me as if I am an idiot. I stub the cigarette out on the steps before even half of it is gone and promise myself I will try again in the afternoon.

It isn't better in the afternoon. I'm just going to have to power through.

MORE RESEARCH

It isn't that hard, I decide a week later. I can do three a day, easy. I feel like an old pro. When I go out on the stoop to smoke, I look for that woman. I imagine she is watching through a window, and I hold the cigarette between my index and middle fingers and tap ash nonchalantly off the side of the steps.

THE DENTIST, TAKE TWO

The dentist says my teeth are doing quite well for a smoker of my caliber. When I ask about my toothache, he says he's not allowed to examine anything else, but the look on my face must be pitiful because he furrows his brow and asks, "Are you okay?"

"Yes. No. My tooth," I say. I am not one of those girls, but things have been going in such a way these past few weeks that I think I am going to start crying.

I chomp on a little piece of sandy paper, and he drills down the fillings in my teeth and then I chomp again. "That's it," he says. "They just weren't quite finished. When they're uneven like that, it's like your whole head is off-balance."

I can't believe that's it, but that's it. My headache starts to fade, the tension leaves my jaw. I click my teeth together with a joy I haven't felt in weeks.

WELL RESEARCHED

How could I have never smoked, not in all twenty-three years of my life? How many hours of work have I spent working when I could have been on a cigarette break? How many friends might I have made, standing around that ashtray, a happy tingle in my brain? How many times (all of those evenings at bars!) have I said no? I must have said no a million times!

With coffee and a cigarette in the morning, I can avoid food until noon. A cigarette after lunch, then one in the midafternoon, and one in the evening. I check the time and think about which cigarette quadrant I'm in. It's like having marking periods, or a job, or a schedule.

QUIT IT! CARA CLINICAL TRIAL: FINE PRINT

To get my $250 I must: seriously try to quit smoking with the help of a nicotine patch, fill out hourly craving and mood charts, attend a support group once a week for two months.

Maybe this isn't worth $250, but I am so thrilled that I've passed the pre-screening that I don't really care. I feel like I've passed an important exam. I myself feel important.

SUPPORT

I am overdressed again, wearing slacks and a blouse. Maybe I am pretending I have a job, even though I don't want one.

In group, I see the attractive guy from my unemployment meeting.

"I recognize you," he says, sitting next to me. "I'm Carlos."

"Hi," I say. "I'm April."

"A month all to yourself," he says. "Ready to give up smoking?"

"Less than I thought I'd be," I admit.

We get our nicotine patches and a packet of poorly photocopied mood and craving charts that remind me of fifth-grade worksheets. The group leader, Nancy, tells us how hard it is to quit smoking. We discuss reasons to stop, personal and otherwise. All of this talk of smoking just makes us all want to go out for a smoke.

OUT

Someone from R & D organizes an unhappy hour for the recently laid off. Even the older employees, men and women with families at home, come out and drink. We laugh about our misery and toast one another and argue about resume formatting, but Jerry, the former head of logistics, starts crying halfway into his second drink, and we take him out of the bar and pat him on the back and remind him that the company can go fuck itself, that essentially it has already gone and fucked itself.

All evening I have been surreptitiously supplying my Long Island iced tea with vodka from a flask to save money at the bar. I have already prepared my room at home, as I often do before I go out, by clearing the path to my bed, closing my blinds, turning down my sheets, and putting a glass of water and two ibuprofen on the nightstand. Today this took longer than usual, what with my bedside accumulation of coffee cups and cereals.

Jeffrey has been standing behind me, talking to Lillie from logistics. I am smiling off into a corner because I'm drunk, but it's nice that it looks as if I've been nursing my drink. "Smoke break?" I hear Jeffrey ask Lillie.

"I'll join you," I announce.

"You don't smoke," says Jeffrey.

"You know everything I do?" I say, and follow them outside.

We stand in a circle puffing. Lillie and Jeffrey glance back and forth at each other, and I look down to be sure I haven't done something stupid, like left toilet paper coming out of my skirt or spilled liquid down my front.

I take a puff, then hold my arm out to the side in a V. "What?" I say.

Jeffrey shrugs, taps at his cigarette. "What's that?" he asks. I look at my shoulder, where my sleeve has moved up just enough to reveal the white corner of a patch.

"A Band-Aid?" I say.

"Is that a nicotine patch?" he says, confused, almost annoyed. "You don't even smoke."

I shrug. More glances between Lillie and Jeffrey, and I realize this is a smoking circle I was not invited to. I crush my cigarette with the toe of my shoe and return to my Long Island iced tea.

IN

I am not very hungover, but I stay in bed most of the next day. I stick on a new nicotine patch, limit myself to one cigarette. I do not limit my coffee intake—I make a full pot and find myself shaking by noon. I eat off-brand Frosted Flakes straight from the box, little bits falling into my bed so that I live in a sandbox. The heat isn't working or is on very low, so I wear a hat and gloves and let the laptop whir on my lap, but it's impossible to get warm. Even the heat of a shower fades the instant I get out of it.

SUPPORT

We look like we are in the same gang, with our nicotine-patched shoulders. "How are you doing?" asks Carlos. "I feel insane sometimes! It's hard." I nod in agreement but feel guilty because I've already had two cigarettes today. They might kick me out if I don't seem to be trying. I don't really think I'm trying.

My hourly mood chart worries me. It looks like a toddler drew zigzags all over it, except that when I look closer, there appears to be a pattern: up every time I smoke, up more every time I drink, and then down down down, below sea level.

MORE SUPPORT

Even better than group is the bar we go to after. Eventually, Carlos and I excuse ourselves and wander a little around the city until he has to catch his train. "We should go out sometime," says Carlos. "I guess we'll have to do something cheap. Or wait until we have jobs."

OPPORTUNITY

It is nice that I can apply to jobs from bed. I look for the wildest jobs I can find in New York, write witty cover letters, and send them out with peppy subject headings: Re: Mycological Assistant—Mushroom lover with strong morel compass; Re: Doggie Blogger—Aspirational dog owner captures voice of a species; Re: Fact-Checker—I've already fact-checked my resume, and I'm your perfect employee. I expect results like I expect lottery winnings.

JEFFREY

"Do you want to come over?" I ask.

"I can't," says Jeffrey.

"Do you want to go out?" I ask.

"I can't," says Jeffrey.

"All right," I say.

"Look, I like you a lot. We've been friends for a year, and we'll still be friends. I didn't know this would happen, but things just happen. I'm kind of seeing Lillie."

I hold my breath for just a second. What is it that you have to do to be kind of seeing someone? Why is no one ever kind of seeing me, even when they are? It is as if I'm unclaimable. I tell myself that it is stupid to care, stupid to be mad. Nobody promised anybody anything.

"And you don't want to ruin that," I say. "You want to see where it goes. I understand."

CARLOS

This time after group, I get plastered. "You okay?" asks Carlos as I sway, looking around for the street I'm supposed to take to my train, but Carlos is wearing a bright yellow shirt that my eyes keep going back to.

"It's a nice shirt," I say.

Next thing I know, we're at my place, and I'm sprawled on my bed and Carlos is at my feet, untying my shoes. "Hey, drink that," he says, pointing to a glass of water on my nightstand.

I drink it, then I try to set my alarm—I don't know why, the days of alarm setting are long gone. I end up knocking over the entire nightstand. "Sorry, sorry," I say as Carlos picks up coffee mugs and pens and that cat journal I've never used.

"I need to go, April," he says. "It's late."

"Do you need to stay?" I say. "The trains? This time of night?"

"No," says Carlos. "Thank you."

"You know what I mean," I say.

"Not tonight," says Carlos. "Another time, maybe."

You never win, I think before I pass out. *It's absolutely impossible to win.*

UNDERSTANDING

I sit hunched on the stoop in the cool blue-gray morning, smoking a cigarette and massaging my temples, thinking of Carlos and Jeffrey. One thing is for sure: I'm not going to tell Rachel about any of this. If you keep stepping in the same ditch over and over, people stop feeling sorry for you because you're either an idiot or a masochist.

I don't understand. I don't understand anything about why people leave, and I don't understand what makes me so leavable. I think this is turning me into a meeker person than I already am, the kind of person who spends relationships spooning coffee grounds quietly into the garbage can, for fear of disturbing the peace.

I wonder if it's different if you do the leaving. Maybe you feel as if you've given something away, rather than lost it. Maybe it's as if it could be yours again, if only you wanted it.

I'm definitely quitting group, I decide as I light a second cigarette with the butt of my first. Maybe I'll even quit smoking. Maybe I'll get a job somewhere far away, in some city I've never visited, in some city where I don't know anyone at all.

THE PORTRAIT

I was born almost completely deaf, and by the time I was seven I had already become a prisoner to my education. In the morning, I had speech therapy and tutoring with Mr. Bishop. We sat at my family's long dining room table, which was always covered with a tablecloth that no one ever saw beneath the mess of books and papers. My mother, who needed reasons to sneak out there and see how I was doing, was often pulling our blue china plates out of the hutch behind us, which is why, when tutoring was over, she and I ate tuna fish sandwiches on our good dishes.

I hated my lessons. Mr. Bishop's lips were fat and smooth like two long, pink party balloons that, it seemed, could be tied into dachshunds at any moment. People think reading lips is a precise skill that just takes practice, like learning Morse code, but it's more of an art, requiring intense concentration paired with context and guesswork. Still, it was nothing compared to the impossible task of learning to speak. I spent lessons resting my hand on the small, humming hill of Mr. Bishop's scratchy throat. My fingers would hover in front of his mouth, feeling for the hot, moist air of his words. I sent my tongue into somersaults, moved my lips in strange ways, pushing the vibrations out of me, adjusting and readjusting to the feedback I found in his face.

My younger brother, Tim, went to all-day kindergarten. He resented that I could wake up late and wear playclothes during the day and that I didn't have to listen to our parents yell. I resented that our mother didn't follow him around everywhere, that his sweaty fist wasn't always stuck in her hand like a bone in its joint. Most of all, I resented that my parents had bought him a new backpack for school. It was covered in geometric neon shapes over a black background and had electric-blue zippers with little corded zipper pulls, plus front, side, and interior pockets, including special compartments for individual pens and other items. The most thrilling part was that it came with a matching lunch box filled with samples of snacks, like Dunkaroos and Pop-Tarts, items my parents wouldn't ordinarily buy. My mother said that when I was speaking and reading well enough, I would be able to go to school and I would get my own backpack and my own lunch box with free snack samples inside.

The backpack was so alluring that I brought a new level of enthusiasm to my lessons, concentrating so hard that I was frequently stricken with headaches. I'd spend post-lesson afternoons lying on the blue corduroy couch in the den, a Ziploc bag full of ice wrapped in a tea towel on my forehead. I'd stare at the stucco ceiling, trying to find shapes and pictures there the way one might look for faces in the clouds.

I quickly realized that even if I didn't have a headache, pretending I did would get me out of my usual afternoon activities, like homework and helping Mom with chores. For a week, I went to the couch directly after lunch and lay there until Tim came home. Tim was towheaded and tiny and his backpack looked like a tortoise shell on him, like something he could have lived inside. He'd fling the thing off next to the stairs, as if it were a burden he was happy to be free of, and then crawl up on the couch and sit on my legs so I'd move them. He'd flip on the TV, *Darkwing Duck* or *TaleSpin*. I couldn't read the lips of cartoon characters, of course, and the black strip of closed-captioning zipped by so fast it might as well have been written in a foreign language. But I watched the pictures, which told most of the story anyway.

My mother didn't let this go on for too long. One day, as I was finishing my pickle spear, she told me we were going to a museum. I watched her say this, her lips like two pieces of ribbon. I shook my head no vigorously—we never went anywhere after tutoring, even when I didn't have a headache—but my mother would not relent.

Before leaving the house, my mother kneeled down in front of me on our colorful stone-tiled entryway and followed her usual routine. First, she dipped two fingers into my front right pants pocket, sober as a doctor taking a pulse, feeling for the laminated information card I carried there in case I got lost. Then she checked my shoelaces, though I'd been tying them myself for a long time, pinching the double knot between her thumb and forefinger. For good measure, she pulled the loops around and through one last time, her lips moving in an incantation I knew by heart: *Bunny ears, bunny ears, jumped in the hole. Popped out the other side, beautiful and bold.* She encouraged me to join her, and when I did her face lit up theatrically. She clapped, saying *Good job! Good job!*

In the cavernous station, we waited hand in hand for the train. The pear trees had just bloomed—they were beautiful but smelled like rotting fish—and little white petals dotted the gray platform like snow. I knew when the train was coming better than anyone. Even before the round lights on the floor blinked, I could feel the vibrations. I would close my eyes and wait for the cool whoosh of air that marked its arrival. On the train, I sat between the window and my mother, my hand finally free of hers. I loved the Metro. As we jetted under the city, I imagined I was an astronaut cast out in the blissful, soundless dark, the silver window of my helmet just a reflection of emptiness and a pinpoint of blue earth below.

When the train slowed at stops, I pressed my hands to the window, waiting for the platform people to appear, some of them slumped down under the weight of luggage, others running frantically, blazers unbuttoned and fluttering behind them like wings. They were trapped out there. I pressed my face to the window and moved my mouth randomly, not forming any words, hoping that someone outside would try to decipher what I was saying.

The museum was a new and terrible torture. My mother read aloud the exhibit labels painstakingly slowly, one after the other, as if the lists of names and years and mediums were the art, her finger bouncing below each word as it passed through her lips, one, two, three times. I tried not to look at the people walking around us, who I thought might be staring, though my mother didn't seem to mind. She stood by the wall, presenting each label the way an elementary school teacher might read a book aloud to a class, except that I was the sole and lonely pupil. Her fingers were long and thin, finished with beautiful French manicured nails, egg-shaped, glossy, and sharp—a fact I knew from the dark crescent grooves they left behind after a sudden grab as I tried to cross the street or run to a swing set.

My escape was sudden and inspired. My mother and I were in the museum bathroom. She liked to use the handicapped stall because we could both fit in it at once, but it was out of order. She read the piece of paper taped to the door as if it were another exhibit label. *Out,* she said. *Out. Out.* Her finger tapped the word three times, then curved under the space, then tapped the next word. *Of. of. of.* And the next. *Order. Order. Order.* She leaned down in front of me, so I could see her lips.

Do you need to use the bathroom? she asked. I shook my head no.

Say it, don't shake it, she said. And I flung my tongue to the roof of my mouth and down again, sending a small *No* up my throat and into the changing O of my lips.

Wonderful! she said, clapping her palms together. She placed my hand on the rounded edge of the sink. *Wait right here. Right here. Understand?*

Just as my mother walked into one stall, a woman walked out of another stall down the line. She washed her hands, glancing at me with pity, as if I were some pet tied to a stop sign in front of a store. I watched my mother's feet splayed in a V under the stall, one of them gently tapping. I figured there was music playing. I lifted my hand from the sink edge, letting it hover just a half inch in the air, a thrilling little retaliation. I put it down, then lifted it instantly again. My hand was still lifted when the woman left the bathroom. Without thought, I darted out behind her.

It was that easy. My heart hammered in my chest, less from nerves than from excitement. The lobby was white and glossy like some great castle hall. It seemed much larger than it had when we'd gone into the bathroom not moments before. I fast-walked to the marble staircase, ascending like a mermaid rising from the depths of the ocean to the sunny surface above.

I felt dreamy and unfurled. The museum was a maze of long legs and clean rooms. A boy in a stroller stuck his tongue out as he passed. His lips moved, and I did not try to read them. I just offered back a blank, fierce stare. Thick gilded frames hung like windows into other worlds: stark women sat in silky gowns, stern men stood in suits, and in a stairwell a dozen Native Americans hung in rows, with fringed robes and feathers splayed above their heads. The people on the walls had gleaming, oily skin and white, human flecks in their eyes. But they were not humans at all, and I was grateful, because they couldn't open their mouths.

I wandered through a stately room with marble floors and thick stone columns, recognizing presidents as I passed, but I only stopped at FDR. I knew him because Mr. Bishop said I should be inspired by his story. His portrait wasn't like the other presidents I'd passed. It looked unfinished, abandoned halfway like most of the pages in my coloring books. There were a bunch of hands lying around at the bottom of the painting, looking severed but animated, speaking without mouths or bodies. Most of the hands seemed nervous, curled in fists or fidgeting with pens, but one in the corner looked friendly, poised in an easy, wrist-flicked way that seemed full of latent energy, as if it were about to spring into action.

I was staring at this hand when I felt a tap on my shoulder. I flipped around to see a stranger bending toward me, asking me a question, her lipsticked lips changing urgently from red to crimson and back as they creviced and flattened, her tongue darting from the dark cave of her mouth like a snake, the white curb of her teeth glistening under the angled museum lights. Again and again and eventually I understood: she wanted to know if I was lost.

This hadn't occurred to me, but of course, I was lost—I didn't know where my mother was or, really, where I was, or how to get home. Automatically, I put my hand in my pocket to feel for the smooth plastic information card. But I didn't pull it out. An image of my brother's backpack flashed before my eyes, and then Mr. Bishop's smile, and my mother's clapping hands, and my own body lying on the couch, stricken down by the intensity of my own efforts.

I would tell her the information myself.

I opened and closed my mouth, at first soundlessly, like testing a hinge, or like a fish caught breathlessly on land.

Then I spoke.

I hadn't even finished a sentence before the woman's face went pale. The skin between her eyebrows furrowed, her nostrils flared, and her top lip just slightly curled. Her eyes were wide, her pupils humongous. At first I thought something hideous had materialized behind me, but no, that wasn't it. It was my voice.

The expression lasted only a few seconds before the woman realized herself.

Oh, she said, her mouth round as the hole in a tube.

I felt heat rise up through my body, into my cheeks and out to my ears, which felt sunburned. I wanted to crawl away from the heat of myself. The whole room must have heard me, every ear, the ears of the woman and the security guard and the tourist couple in the corner and even the ears of the portraits themselves.

I thought of the hours of lessons, I thought of words and all that were part of them: the shape of the lips, the twist of the tongue, the pattern of breath, the pulses, the quivers, the throbs, and finally, after everything, the meaning, which, even if it were pronounced and produced correctly, might be, in the end, a lie or misunderstood. My mother had lied, Mr. Bishop had lied, the backpack was a lie, each piece of encouragement was a bread crumb thrown out on a path leading me here, to this lonely place, a mansion of cold marble where I was not welcome and didn't belong.

The woman looked embarrassed now too. She was still bending toward me, still talking, but I couldn't see what she was saying. Her head was turned slightly, as if she were conferring with one of the portraits. She was over-enunciating, her lips stretching into incomprehensible shapes.

I put my hands on this woman's stupid cheeks, twisting her face toward mine, so that we were eye to eye, so that maybe I could see what she was saying. But she jerked her head from my hands, and then looked back at me with an expression of disgust that, this time, she didn't try to hide. As if it were my own fault that twice now I hadn't been the girl she'd expected.

The card in my pocket felt stiff against my thigh. I closed my eyes, but the world did not disappear—I could still feel my own heat and the heat of the woman, the smell of her sweat mixed with perfume, something floral and too sweet, but more than that I could still see her face, hanging before me in the darkness, framed in gold and finished with horrified, white-flecked eyes.

How to wait

Prepare yourself haphazardly.

For example, get a dog. You may think you want a large dog who will growl at strangers, bark at robbers, chase down assailants, but what you really want is a small dog that will sit on the furniture, lie on your lap, sleep in your bed, that will love you endlessly, that will forget about all of the things you forget, like to take him for walks, fill his water bowl, feed him every day. Name him a thinly disguised version of your husband's name. For example, if your husband's name is Richard, name him Dick Tracy. If your husband's name is William, name him Billy the Kid.

Complete daily visualization exercises. Imagine the white desolation of a half-empty bed. Imagine that he is so thoroughly gone that even the depression he leaves when he gets up to use the bathroom is gone, even his toothbrush is gone, stored away in the medicine cabinet, dry-bristled, waiting, like you.

Make lists. You will need these later. For example, a to-do list: paint the bedrooms blue, paint the nightstand white, paint the family room cream, paint the kitchen eggshell, retile the bathroom gray, get new comforters to match the new walls, get a new shower curtain to match the new tiles, get new towels to match the new shower curtain.

When he comes home with the date, you will know. He will hang up his black raincoat. It will be raining and his raincoat will be black and inside it he will be as white as a tissue. He will not quite look at you. You will kiss him on the cheek and he will turn his head, just slightly, and ask if you've moved the chair in the living room. When he is gone, you will probably move a lot of things. You will move everything. Everything will be moved. When he returns you will try to kiss him and he will turn his head and say, You moved everything.

Decide that you will not move everything. Decide that you will move nothing. Start a new to-do list: join the gym, join a book group, make the photo albums you have meant to make every year for the past five years, make a pie that doesn't run.

Call his mother for the recipe for strawberry-rhubarb pie. It is the one thing she can make perfectly that you cannot seem to make at all. You will soon have the time to fix your mistakes.

Speaking of pies: besides them, what will you eat? Get a cookbook called *Cooking for One*. There are several things that might go wrong if you don't. You might eat only eggs and ramen noodles and runny pies for weeks on end. Or you might prepare the usual amount of spaghetti, the usual amount of quiche, the usual amount of chicken Parmesan. You might have to buy new Tupperware, which you might have to throw away when everything goes bad.

Know that what is coming could be even worse than what you know is coming, but do not attempt to know any further. Do not think: *The Deer Hunter, Apocalypse Now, Saving Private Ryan.* Do not think: *All Quiet on the Western Front, Slaughterhouse-Five, The Red Badge of Courage.* Do not think: My Lai, the bombing of Dresden, bags full of ears.

Devour Buddhist poetry like fortune cookies: *Empty your mind of all thoughts. Don't grieve. Anything you lose comes round in another form.*

Do not listen to that goddamned song "Christmas in the Trenches."

Let your stomach ache. Call this feeling a stomachache. Make up reasons why it has developed: you are sensitive to spicy food, you drink too much soda, there is a flu going around.

When you hear phrases like *high risk of death or capture,* think instead of trite phrases about liberty, even if they come directly from pickup truck bumper stickers: FREEDOM ISN'T FREE, SUPPORT OUR TROOPS. You will soon be a cliché yourself, condensed into symbols. You will wear an American flag on your collar and a yellow ribbon on your breast and one, also, on the back of your car. You will say the Pledge of Allegiance in the morning, even the part about God, and you will put your hand on your heart. You will mean it. You will mean all of it.

Memorize every part of him. Memorize the thick, toned bulk of his arms and legs, the muscular rises and falls of his abdomen, the territory you have known for years, have learned by heart but not, until now, by rote. Memorize the positions of his freckles, dots like soldiers staked out across the sand of a desert map. Memorize the curve of each fingernail, white splinters of nascent moons. Memorize the uncommon crinkle in the fleshy part of his ear, a perfect imperfection, a detail you have always believed your children would inherit.

Do not crave the expanding bud of a crinkle-eared baby in your aching stomach, a flower that will not wilt for at least eighteen years.

Confuse "marital" and "martial." Go commando. Advance. Seize. Incite invasion.

When you hear him whimpering quietly in the night, turned away from you, put your arm over him and feel for the wet of his eyelashes, the dampness of his cheeks. He has comforted you this way many times. He has always done this for you.

In the dark blackness of rolling credits, wait for him to tell you that he doesn't mind dying, he just doesn't want you to hate him for choosing to go. He'll say, over and over: *If I die, it will be my own fault, and you'll hate me.* He'll say: *I just don't want you to hate me.*

Tell him over and over that you could never hate him. Tell him so many times that you do not know what you're saying, the words dropping like blanks from your soft, civilian tongue.

He will get louder. He will wail like a dog, like a baby, like a ghost. He has cried only once before, at your wedding. He was crying because he loved you and when you walked down the aisle you were the most beautiful thing he had ever seen. There is no use being modest about this. He is crying for essentially the same reason now.

You have cried many times in your life. You cried when your parents were going to split up, and again when they got back together. You cried when your sister went to college and when your brother decided not to go. You have cried everywhere: in bathrooms, on roller coasters, in traffic jams, in the seats of movie theaters playing romantic comedies that received mediocre reviews. But you do not cry now.

Get a second dog. Several things could happen to the first. For example, he could get run over by a car. For example, he could escape out the door when you're carrying in the groceries. For example, he could get sick, you could drop him on his head, he could be stolen by a jealous neighbor.

Do not read the news. Do not watch the news. Do not go to the *New York Times,* looking for statistics. Do not spend hours examining the faces of the dead.

Do not try to decide what war this is, whose war this is. This is not part of the equation you are working on.

Think about what he said in your first month together, his bare arms wrapped around you like vines. He said: *I'm afraid I will wake and not know it's you.* He said: *I'm afraid I will snap your neck.* Even then, fatigued and in love, he was ready for war.

Donate to, but do not look at, the man with one leg, staked out at a VA table set up like an ambush at the front of the grocery store.

Do not try to cherish every moment. This will only ruin every moment. Know that there are things you will miss, lose, wish for longingly in the night, but do not think about what these things are, do not think about the ways in which you will not know him anymore.

Go out together. Drink like a man, like a warrior, like a soldier on leave. You are strong, you are belligerent, you are tears, you are vomit, you are a rock, a rack, Iraq, a desert, dehydrated, desiccated, desolate. He will lead you home peacefully, wordlessly, as if you hadn't spilled sauce on your shirt, broken your wineglass, stolen a pork chop for the dogs. He will hold you steady in a way that you cannot possibly hold yourself.

When you go to bed that night, all tears and vomit and snot, he will wipe your face as if you could produce only pure water. He will soon do much more for people he loves much less. And at night, he will wake up alone, in not quite the body you have memorized, changed now by sun and sand, in a bed so small there is no empty space where you should be.

UNATTACHED

I was out for a run, neck to ankle in pink and black spandex, and for a single, happy moment, I felt sleek as a scuba diver. Running was a new hobby I liked to blame on Dylan. When things end poorly, I write lists of lessons I have learned, changes to make, et cetera. Incidentally, I have a lot of lists, mini spiral steno pads full of them, stacked under the bed. After Dylan left, I'd resolved to run daily. I'd gotten the idea from googling something stupid, something like "relationship failure not connecting." The goal was to feel every part of myself as the human/animal it's supposed to be, as muscles and lungs, as feet on pavement, grounded, because I was having that problem again, connecting.

And it was working, maybe, sometimes. In small spurts of letting go, the hot burn in my lungs would feel like fuel instead of fire, and I'd be off, springing down the stone-gray sidewalk, pretending the scenery was blurring by, a Monet of lime-green and yellow grass and brown brick town houses. And then it would be over, and I'd be tired again, my chest heaving, and I'd begin to worry about the things that can befall a person while running, while being outdoors, while being a woman: rape, murder, relentless ridicule that cuts to the bone.

What did befall me, in the end, was none of these things.

That day, the sky was awesome, like some high-saturation desktop background, bright and empty save for a single, cartoonish cloud. An exhilarating tingle hung in the air, like the shift in energy before a storm (negative ions, Dylan always said).

I was making a list in my head that had nothing to do with self-improvement (milk, eggs, tuna, peanut butter) when the hairs on my arm stood straight up. My stomach dropped, that belly-flip feeling like when your car takes the crest of a hill at just the right speed, and as I tried to run, I realized my feet weren't on the ground. I was floating (falling?) toward a tree whose branches had been, just moments before, directly and safely above my head. By some instinct I'm glad to know I have, I grabbed on to a branch while the rest of my body headed onward toward the sky in a sort of slo-mo somersault.

Well, shit, I thought. There are lots of things you imagine you'll do in a crisis, but there isn't much you *can* do while hanging from a tree, legs shooting sneaker first into a pit of blue sky, looped shoelaces dangling in the direction of the sun. I felt like a piece of postmodern art, photoshopped somehow into this predicament.

In theory, I was upside down, but no blood rushed to my head. I felt light and buoyant. It was as if gravity had not only reversed, but also weakened. I inched my hands along the branch, recalibrating my movements to contend with the extra float, and wrapped myself tight around the tree trunk like a cartoon bear. My head was pointing toward the grass of someone's lawn.

Around me, everything that had been unattached was either going or gone, ascending (falling?) toward the heavens like escaped helium balloons drifting casually away from the earth—ants and acorns, leaves and dirt, flowers and terra-cotta pots and lawn gnomes and lawn mowers and children's toys, like a dirty blue and yellow plastic slide, the kind I remember playing on as a kid. A Wiffle ball clinked out of a gutter. A black hose rose like a charmed snake up the length of a house and hovered there. Cars that had been parked along the sidewalk or in driveways moments earlier were already hitting the stratosphere. One disappeared into that fat cloud near the sun. I heard a whimper: was it me? But no, in the distance I caught sight of a family dog spinning through the sky.

I felt nauseous because my brain kept flipping the picture, reinterpreting which way was up. When I saw the world as upside down, then the houses and trees were like stalactites hanging from the ceiling of earth above my head, and our little civilization was very small, just the tiniest inhabited layer in a world made up almost entirely of air.

Soon the sky cleared, save the occasional flower that suddenly popped out of the dirt and drifted away, or a leaf, like the orange-brown one that detached from a branch just a foot from my head. I fought the urge to reach out and grab it. Instead I watched it fall away, kept watching it, straining my eyes until I lost it to the grain of vision. I listened for the dog, but it too had disappeared.

By now, I'd shimmied down a little to sit on a branch, though I didn't dare let go of the trunk. The air smelled of overturned earth. A golden midafternoon light, the kind only possible in late fall, shone through the brown and red leaves in my tree, making them look like the final standing shards of a shattered stained glass window. A serene dreaminess overwhelmed me, the sort of peace I imagined people felt when they had conceded to death.

I thought about calling for help, but it didn't seem appropriate. After all, I wasn't the only one in a predicament. Besides, I'm not an inspired yeller. It's one of my flaws, really, and the reason I quit karate in the fourth grade after getting only a yellow belt. It was the reason I only whispered "Whoopsie" one summer day when I fell sideways while wearing a wedge sandal and sprained my ankle, walking on the foot for a week before seeing a doctor, and why I felt embarrassed when my mom screamed in the middle of a Walgreens after learning her sister had gotten hit by a delivery truck while trying to cross the street in Midtown, and why I didn't cry at the funeral or any of the days before or after, and why my own sister whispered in my ear in the middle of an echoing church, "What the fuck is wrong with you?"

It's strange how calm I am in a crisis, because I'm afraid of everything. I'm afraid of people: waiters, tech support, pizza delivery guys, coworkers, even the people I'm supposed to know. I'm also afraid of transportation: planes, subways, trains, buses, cars, elevators. Also, invisible things: carbon monoxide, those brain-eating amoebas found in lakes. I am farseeing, a chess player calculating all of fate's possible moves. Expect the Unexpected! is my motto, but even in the many, detailed, and wild scenarios my brain has conjured, I never expected this.

The breakup with Dylan? That I expected. I braced myself for it from the moment we met, and even so I let him nestle in, like a worm inching its way into the heart of a rotting apple. Symbiosis began to occur. He brought me half-price lunch from Bubba's on Wednesday afternoons: a giant burger, well-done, plus two surprise sides of his choosing. He cleaned off my perpetually finger-printed glasses with a magic combination of his warm breath and whichever cotton T-shirt he was wearing. He was a member of a community woodshop, and he kept asking me what I wanted him to make me. "I don't know?" I kept answering. "Whatever you want?"

Dylan claimed that my rising intonation was a defense against commitment. "I don't think so?" I said. "Maybe I just talk like this? Maybe our whole generation just talks like this?" What was I supposed to tell him? That he was right? That I actually liked my IKEA furniture? That I took comfort in its smooth, laminate look, in the pleasant feeling it gave me, a longing for some made-up version of Scandinavia? That one day we would break up and I wouldn't want furniture that would remind me of him?

In the end, he made me a corner shelf for my most impossible corner and a media cabinet that perfectly held my TV and peripherals. Just as I feared, they were so flawlessly tailored to my life that I could never get rid of them.

In the night, Dylan looked like the outline of a person I might not know.

"You asleep?" he would ask when he was almost out.

"Definitely," I'd answer.

He'd kiss me, and I'd forget to kiss back.

"Where are you?" he would ask.

I was in one of a million places: I was the ghostly figure in the gray-dust aftermath of a subway bombing; I was the eviscerated human hanging from a shattered passenger-side window; I was a bodega shopper shot and losing blood next to a display of Cheetos.

Where am I supposed to be? I would think, but I'd say, "Nowhere?"

I wrote this on the list of things I'd learned: *The answer is "here." That's always where you're supposed to be.*

The temperature was dropping. Or maybe I was just cold because I wasn't running anymore. I tried to stop thinking about Dylan. I tried to just be *mindful,* a skill I was learning from a meditation podcast. Or was trying to learn between advertisements for box subscriptions, where you get overpriced samples of snacks and clothes delivered directly to your door. I was supposed to think about what my body parts were feeling, but this usually led me into a panic, because I'd focus a lot on my teeth, which were always on the brink of decay. This time, though, I skipped the teeth entirely and went right to my hands, which were holding on to the tree so tightly that they were starting to ache. I gave each a rest in turn, shaking out one hand and then the other. The bark had left an imprint on my skin that I watched fade as I bent my fingers back and forth.

A voice, suddenly, was calling out to me: "Excuse me! Hello!" I flung my head toward the town house—whoever was yelling, I was in their lawn.

It was a woman with a white fluff of hair. She stood in the open doorway, two stories of house and a pointed roof and a blue sky pitched below her.

Behind her, papers were scattered on her ceiling, which was now the floor, and a wooden table was legs up, like a dead bug. A bald man bounced into view, like an astronaut on the moon. He seemed to be enjoying himself. "Mass and distance!" I heard him shouting. "Mass and distance!"

"Are you okay?" the woman called. I envied that she was able to sound concerned while yelling. Sometimes I had difficulty establishing appropriate volume and tone during conversations, especially with people I didn't know. "Just be yourself," Dylan had recommended. But what if I already was just being myself?

Just be yourself? I had written on the list. Then I'd scribbled out the question mark. Later, when reviewing the list, I put it back in.

"Fine, thanks," I croaked back to the woman, too quietly, then louder and too aggressively: "Yes! Thanks!"

"Would you like to come in?" the woman called.

I made an awkward little laughing noise, because this seemed impossible, because I was sitting in a tree about twenty feet from this woman's front door. I opened my mouth and closed it again, trying and failing to think of an appropriate response.

"Hold on!" she shouted, and then she closed the door and disappeared. I waited in the tree, trying to be mindful about my body, except not my hands or my teeth.

Just as I began to wonder if the woman had been a figment of my imagination, her door swung open and she reappeared, a thick hemp rope clutched in her fist. I had to wonder what sort of person just happened to have a length of rope on hand. Then I thought of what might befall me if I stayed outside: nightfall, hypothermia, starvation, floating into oblivion.

Standing in that doorway, she seemed, somehow, poised over a precipice at the edge of the world, like a superhero or a character in a children's book, like maybe if she tipped out of the doorway she would fly instead of fall.

"I'm going to throw this to you!" she shouted. She announced everything as she did it, like a friendly nurse. She tried to lasso the rope out to me, but it just flailed around the entryway and doorframe. The man appeared again, grabbed it from her without a word, and flung the rope out like a fishing line, which worked surprisingly well. It snaked toward me and I caught it— one-handed!—and all three of us cheered as the rope bristled in my palm.

"As an extra precaution, my husband is also tying our end to the banister," the woman said. I hoped he'd been a scout or a sailor or soldier or some other profession where you learn to tie knots.

I triple-wrapped the rope around my waist before tying it because I am not a scout or a sailor or soldier, and recently I'd learned—from a YouTube video, no less—that I'd been tying my shoelaces wrong for years.

Was I starting to feel a little heavier? As if to confirm this, the husband jumped with what appeared to be reduced bounce. "Best to do it now, perhaps," said the woman. The man hustled up behind her to hold on to the rope. "We're ready!" she shouted.

I looked down into the blue abyss below, my heart racing. I

felt like I was standing on top of a Looney Tunes high dive. How strong were these people? How heavy was I? How sturdy was this rope? How firm was my grip?

"Go!" she shouted.

I stopped thinking. I went. I slipped off the branch as if I were simply slipping into a hot tub, but instead I fell into the sky. I was like a tethered astronaut or a baby on an umbilical cord. The cool air rushed past my cheeks, the tree grew small below me, its leaves fluttering gently like hundreds of fingers waving goodbye.

At my peak, dangling above the town houses, I had an unbelievable view. Streets ran toward the horizon in parallel lines, empty-looking neighborhoods set out between them in squares and rectangles. Pointed roofs in red, gray, and brown jutted from the ground like giant arrows pointing toward the sky.

As the couple reeled me in, I bumped up against the tiny attic window, the brick facade, a second-story window where I saw a bed upside down on the ceiling, mattress on the floor, splayed quilt pinned below it. Then there I was, at the top of the doorframe, the woman looking at me from above, her face flushed red from exertion. I climbed inside the house and the woman stretched her hands out toward me like a mother about to embrace her wobbling toddler. I reached back the exact same way, and we shared a hug that felt weirdly natural.

When she placed her hands on my shoulders, I realized I was shaking. She straightened her arms and looked at my face in a grandmotherly way, or maybe I was just getting that vibe from the mothy-menthol smell of the house. "There," she said gently. Like saying, "You're safe." Her skin was mottled and wrinkly and her cheeks had a jowly droop, but her eyes looked friendly. Of course, you never knew.

The woman introduced herself as Rosa. Her husband was Harry.

"I'm Kesha," I said even though that's not my name.

In the center of the room, a ceiling fan whirred in a circle-blur of brown, and the metal chain pull kept getting swept up over and over again in the blades, clicking in and out and getting stuck again. The pale bulbs in the fan's tulip-shaped frosted glass shades tilted up from the ground like stage lights, and I made the mistake of looking directly at a bulb, so that even when I looked away, a dark cutout in the shape of a bulb punctured my vision.

Hanging on the wall—some upside down, some perfectly rotated on their nails—were framed diplomas, a half dozen white porcelain crosses, family photos from the seventies featuring younger versions of Rosa and Harry as well as three smiling kids who, photo by photo, kept growing up. Green shaggy wall-to-wall carpeting, spiked and matted in different spots, was affixed above us. It made me feel as if we were huddled in a mossy cave. Outside, the grass looked like a low, carpeted sky.

"Would you like something to drink, Kesha?" Rosa asked.

"I'm okay," I said.

"Maybe it's a good idea to stay hydrated," Rosa suggested.

"What the girl needs is a whiskey," said Harry.

"Anything is fine," I offered.

"Why don't we get comfortable?" Rosa said after she'd gathered the drinks. "No use waiting around to see what rusts."

I helped flip over some furniture. Rosa sat on the dark red velvety couch and I on a mustard-colored love seat that was surprisingly cozy despite the sunken seat. The drinks—OJ for the gals, whiskey for Harry—were served in fancy highball glasses with gold trim, remarkably unchipped after the flip.

Harry was still up and trying to bounce. He didn't go very far. Gravity seemed to have settled into its new orientation with its standard Earthly pull. "Perhaps you arrived in the nick of time," said Rosa. Harry looked like a kid whose balloon had floated away. He slumped down next to Rosa.

"So, what do we think happened here?" asked Rosa, looking out the window.

I shrugged at the same time Harry shouted, "This is impossible! If gravity has reversed, then the weight of the air alone...! The oxygen! As the distance between objects *decreases,* or rather *increases*... What I mean is, you have to consider the *mass*..." He was stumbling over his words, angry at himself for not being able to articulate what he couldn't remember.

"It *does* seem impossible," Rosa agreed. "He used to be a physics professor, you know," she said to me.

"Cool beans," I said. *Cool beans?*

I glanced back at the photos on the wall, featuring Harry when he was a physics professor with hair. I could already tell who'd gotten the raw end of this deal.

"Neat highball glasses," I added, too loudly, to fill the silence.

"These were wedding gifts nearly fifty years ago, if you can believe it," Rosa said. I didn't hear a trace of regret in her voice.

For some reason, I made the sign of the cross. "Impressive," I said.

I *was* impressed. Even fifty months of dating was unfathomable to me. How long did it take to settle into the idea that a person was going to stay, and then move on to worrying about something else, like when they were going to die—or worse, go crazy?

Were long relationships really like an old pair of shoes, as people said? I thought of them as more like old anti-slip shower mats: bright and clean at the beginning but with mildew growing beneath ever since suctioning in place on day one. By the time you saw the mildew creeping up on top, the bottom was already infested beyond repair. You had to either tear out the mat and get used to slipping or keep it and get used to a lifetime of ignoring what was obviously disgusting.

"Why don't we play a game?" suggested Rosa. "What do you like?"

"The one with the words," said Harry. This was not, I guessed, Harry's most strategic choice.

"Scrabble," said Rosa.

"That's right," said Harry.

"I love Scrabble," said Rosa.

When we opened the Scrabble box, all the letters were already flipped over to the blank side. "Well, that's something," Rosa said.

Dylan and I had played Scrabble once. I'd won by a lot, but otherwise it hadn't ended well. Dylan hadn't wanted to play in the first place because he thought the game would be uneven, that I had a much better vocabulary than he did and thus was sure to win. I told him my vocabulary wasn't all that good. "In fact," I'd said, "it's so bad that I can't even think of a word better than 'bad' to describe it."

"Don't just let me win," said Dylan. I didn't, but when the game was over, Dylan was angry. "I guess you were wrong about your vocabulary," he said.

"Well, the game is about math, really," I replied.

"You told me you were terrible at that too!"

"It's all just luck," I said finally, and I felt like I was trying to get out of several lies I hadn't even meant to tell.

"You're impossible," he said. I was turning him into someone who clenched his teeth.

"But I'm so flexible?" I answered.

"You trying not to create problems," he said angrily, "is creating problems." He stood up. "You're like a puppet," he said. "You puppet yourself around, like you're your own marionette, like you're a ventriloquist." He'd run out of puppets to call me. "What are you trying to avoid?" he asked. "Everything, actually," he answered. "You're trying to avoid everything."

He walked out of the room, and I saw that Dylan was right, that in the very process of trying to stop the spread of mildew, I was always spreading it faster.

Scrabble with Rosa and Harry was more successful than it had been with Dylan. Not only was I winning, but neither Rosa nor Harry seemed to mind.

When it was Harry's turn, Rosa would mull over his letters with him. "Oh, how lucky," she might say, "you have an *ED*." Or "Two *E*s always pair well." Or, pointing at the board, "Well, perhaps I shouldn't have left that triple open for you to nab."

"Okay, okay," he would say eventually, waving her away, "I've got it!" He'd put the word down, beaming, as if it had been his idea all along. But he knew. "Bravo!" Rosa would say, and Harry would put his hand on her knee, thanking her.

As we played, the late afternoon light shone through the two naked windows as if from a glowing sea. I felt a certain kind of coziness seep into me. I was reminded of snow days when I was young, when a storm had taken out the power and we were giddy with the crisis, gathering flashlights and candles and fleece blankets. After that, all we could do was wait. My mother, sister, and I would lie on the carpet by the light of the sliding glass doors and play Monopoly, watching the snow fall. If I looked out the window just right, I could get the sensation that the snow was static, that it was me who was moving, as if I were in a spaceship shooting through stars.

In those moments, nothing else mattered, not the petty details of existence, like homework and the dishes, and not the bigger ones either, like my parents' impending divorce and whether or not I would manage to do anything worthwhile with my time on the overheating planet. How safe I'd always felt, nestled in the soft aftermath of catastrophe, protected, finally, from the terror and exhaustion of anticipating disaster.

Was this why Rosa was happy? Misfortune had already arrived: the person she'd chosen to spend her life with was losing his mind. Or maybe she was just someone who moved forward no matter the conditions, as if life were a train constantly being rerouted, as if she never expected to arrive anywhere in particular, as if she just appeared places and thought, *Ah, what do we do here?*

I was about to place my next word when the Scrabble letters

began to float off the board. I felt a strange tingle, a certain lightness, and once again I was not on the ground.

We descended from the ceiling to the floor without incident, the furniture and tables bumping back into the ground, the photographs rotating on their nails. The Scrabble letters fell too, all around us, and I hoped they would land in some configuration that would offer a clue about how to proceed, some secret key I needed to add to my list so that I could do everything better next time. But they just scattered around the room. There was no way to put the board back together as it had been.

I should've been relieved that things were returning to normal, but instead my heart felt tight, as if a small animal had balled up in my chest. Harry, on the other hand, was enthusiastic. He pulled himself up off the ground and shot his fist into the air. "Yes!" he shouted.

We watched from the window as a gentle rain of objects returned to earth: cars and cats, flowers and toys. Across the street, a car landed in the driveway as if it had been parked there all along. Then the sky was clear, save for a dramatic fluorescent cloud, a deep pinky-orange, trimmed in a murky shadow.

I felt heavy, heavier than when I'd started out, but Rosa was moving at the usual rate, picking up tiles from the shaggy green carpet and tossing them into the cardboard box. "Stay as long as you need, Kesha," Rosa said.

But I didn't stay—it was getting dark, anyway. I left the house without looking back, sprinting by the time I passed the mailbox. I was starting to worry that this would happen again, that I'd float away, that I wouldn't be able to come back down.

THE LUNATIC REPORT

The truth is, when I started as a Junior Volunteer, I wanted someone rolled out of the hospital dead. I didn't wish anyone dead,
but if someone did die, I wanted to be there to see it like on
television, where everyone rushes for the metal paddles and yells,
"Clear!" Something less dramatic, even, would have sufficed: a
quiet breath, a long, last beep. But instead of metal paddles and
long beeps I refilled glove boxes and folded blankets, made beds
with hospital corners, and poured water into cups for old men
who winked long winks and asked if I had a boyfriend.

Sometimes I walked past the mental health wing, down the
stairs, and into the basement, a labyrinth where the hospital's
pristine whiteness had been worn to gray. The medical records
were in corridor D, where the hallways were stacked with forms.
Exposed tube lights let off an unearthly glow, casting sharp,
unattractive shadows under the eyes and noses of the people who
worked down there—troglodytes, I called them.

I spent hours in the basement each week, organizing emergency room intake forms, placing them, for reasons never revealed to me, in reverse-numerical order. I chose this boring task because of the Lunatic Report. This was the name I'd given the pile of intake forms marked MENTAL HEALTH, which I'd separate out to read at the end of my shift.

Technically, I wasn't allowed to read the confidential forms, but even more technically, I, like all Junior Volunteers, wasn't allowed in the mental health wing. This had been a big disappointment— one not revealed to me until after twenty hours of volunteer training. I thought of the Lunatic Report as a kind of consolation prize.

Reading the report was a thrill, like when you drive through a neighborhood at night, and the windows of some houses are bright, curtains opened, and you can make out the families inside, doing what families do, like sit around at the dinner table passing the peas.

Among the binge drinkers and bulimics were the true stars of the report: a woman who heard voices like radio static, a man who claimed to be a vampire after being bitten by a flying squirrel.

The hospital took care of Thursdays and Fridays, but there were still three other afternoons to get through. Mondays and Wednesdays, I played intramural soccer—I wasn't any good, and I spent most of the scrimmages rubbing at the sprayed-on white lines in the grass with the toe of my sneaker. Tuesday was a problem, and after failing to become an upstanding member of the play's crew or the yearbook, I joined the Write Stuff, the only remaining option, and one I'd originally nixed because of its name, which had been voted democratically into existence by the group itself.

The Write Stuff had five members, all girls: a semi-goth chronicling the life of a centaur named Elzebar and four others who wrote about their crushes and who melded together in my mind like a soup. The group's adviser was the home ec teacher, Ms. Barnes.

The premise of the club was simple. Every other week, we wrote a story and read it aloud to the group. That was it. We sat on stools at a long table among the seventies dark orange and avocado green kitchens in the home ec room, eating pretzels and drinking Diet Coke out of the unbreakable home ec dishware.

I put off writing my first story until the night before it was due. I sat at the wood table in my room, which I used for a desk, staring at an empty legal pad until the lines began to blur and pulse. I felt a rush of respect for the girls in my group, even if their stories sucked. Outside my window, a single star shone in the sky like a stray piece of glitter. Maybe it was a planet. After a while there was nothing else to look at, and I put my pen to paper and began to write.

I started my story with something I'd read in the Lunatic Report: an anorexic woman tried to kill herself by taking a bottle of aspirin because, she said, she was angry at her boyfriend for trying to "fatten her up." In my version, the boyfriend sends the anorexic woman flowers in the hospital—or so he thinks. It is, in fact, an Edible Arrangement. The instant the woman sees it, she jumps out the window.

When I looked up from reading this story, my club mates were looking down at their notebooks, pretending to be interested in something they'd written there. Finally the semi-goth looked up at me with her charcoal-encircled eyes and said, "That was weird."

After group, Ms. Barnes pulled me aside. She was youngish and always wore dresses with puffed sleeves that I imagined she sewed herself, but then I saw one in a Delia's catalog. I braced myself for the sort of finger wagging that had resulted in me ditching the play crew and the yearbook staff. But what she said was, "You know, you should consider applying for honors English next year."

"Why?" I asked. Maybe, because she was a home ec teacher, she didn't understand who qualified for honors English.

"Well, I'm not saying you're Shakespeare," she said, "but there is something kind of clever happening."

Regardless of her qualifications, it put me in a good mood. That afternoon, I arrived home on the late bus, dropped the mail on the counter, snatched a snack pudding from the fridge, and took the steps two at a time to the guest room.

"Dad? You up?" I asked, peeking in. The room was dark, lights off and shades drawn. My father was facing away from the door, sheets crumpled around his waist. The white sheets matched his white undershirt, and for the moment it took my eyes to adjust, he seemed to be just limbs and a head. The room smelled like dirty gym clothes.

"Headache again?" I asked, flipping on the overhead light and taking a spoonful of pudding.

"Ouch," he said, putting his elbow over his eyes so I could see the yellow armpit stain on his undershirt. "And *still*, not *again*."

"Hmm?"

"You mean that I *still* have a headache, not that I have a headache *again*," he said. "Turn it off, please." He'd had a headache for weeks, ever since they downsized at the construction company where he'd worked for over a decade. He lay down in the guest room the day he had been laid off, and he hadn't really gotten up since. Sometimes I'd bring him food—scrambled eggs, eggs over easy, eggs in the hole, whatever we'd learned to make in home ec.

I flipped off the overhead light and clicked on the little wrought iron lamp next to the bed, which had a stained glass shade that splayed dark blue and green and purple across the wall, like some forbidding seascape. I had once occupied this room, and the walls were still pink, accented with a border of stenciled brown bunnies and pink hearts.

"Maybe you could, like, get up and take a walk," I suggested. "Do a little karate or something?" I threw a few fake punches into the air, gripping the spoon in my fist.

"Well, you seem happy," he said. He rolled toward me, and a triangle of purple hit his eye. His brown hair was matted completely to one side of his head, forming a half Mohawk. My dad's wide-set eyes reminded me of dots on the back of a butterfly's wings. Sometimes, when his eyes went blank, it seemed as if they might fly off his face, leaving just two smooth patches of skin behind.

The most surprising result of my father's time in bed was his beard. I had never seen him with one, but now the bottom half of his face was covered in an uneven mess of wiry brownish-red hair speckled with gray, which made him seem a decade older than he had been not a month before.

I sat on the edge of my father's bed, the way he used to sit on the edge of mine when he came home from work late at night, smelling of sweat and sawdust. "You've got a genius-child on your hands," I said. "Just thought you should know."

"Oh yeah?" The corners of his mouth bent up in a strained almost-smile. I took the opportunity and attempted to force the rest of my pudding snack on him, but he pushed it back to me.

"Teacher thinks I should try for honors English next year," I said.

"You're not in it this year?"

"Of course I am," I said—because why not? "It's just, she thinks I'm *so* brilliant that I should be in it *every* year."

"That's great," he said. "How'd you get to be so impressive?"

I shrugged. "Just decided to be. That's all."

On Friday, I was shoving plastic gloves into glove boxes on 2C when I saw a priest walk onto the floor. I followed him because I thought he might be there to say prayers before a death, and maybe I'd get to see a body rolled out. When I walked into the room he'd gone into, the priest turned to me. He looked at my ugly, bright red Junior Volunteer vest, at the giant VOLUNTEER pin stuck to it, and then said with a smile, "There are a lot of good teenagers out there today."

"Thanks," I said. I hated the word "teenager." It made me think of pimples and after-school specials about periods and peer pressure. I asked the lady—middle-aged, rosy cheeks—if she wanted me to refill her water.

"Could you bring me some applesauce?" she asked, very

chipper. "And ginger ale? If you wouldn't mind?" These were not, I knew, dying wishes.

When I was on my way back from delivering the lady her afternoon snack, one of the nurses asked if I could feed Jell-O to the man in room 257. "He's going to hit on you," she said, "but don't worry, his hands are tied down."

The man in room 257 was ancient, with dry, cracked lips and concave cheeks that gave him a shrunken-head look. Tufts of gray hair sprouted from his ears like grass from a potted plant. His wrists were braceleted in leathery brown cuffs with silver buckles, which wrapped around him almost twice because his wrists were so thin. His heavy breathing sounded like snoring. I couldn't believe my luck. He wasn't even in the mental health wing, but I felt as if a real-life file from the Lunatic Report had opened before me.

"They've got me tied up in this shit," he said in a hoarse voice, raising one arm an inch off the bed and then plopping it back down again. "No wonder I can't feed myself!"

I just stood there, forgetting to speak.

The man sighed loudly. "You just gonna stand there or what?"

"Oh," I said, remembering myself. "I've got some Jell-O. Strawberry."

"Strawberry my ass," he said. "That shit tastes like cough syrup."

"You don't have to eat it."

"How old are you?"

"Fifteen," I said, pulling the Saran Wrap off the little pink bowl.

"You're pretty," he said. "You're very beautiful. I mean that."

"Thanks. Do you want some Jell-O or not?"

He shrugged, and I pressed the button on the side of his bed, whirring him slowly to a sitting position. I started spooning Jell-O into his mouth, slowly, bite by bite, except there was no actual *biting,* since he didn't have any teeth.

He stretched out his pinky as far as he could to graze my thigh. "You are very pretty."

I stepped back but kept feeding him, leaning over him awkwardly. I was trying to take note of some things about him for another story, the kind of details you just can't get from a Lunatic Report, like the Pine-Sol smell of the room mixed with his BO, and the way his saggy arm skin looked like a costume for his bones.

"What? Give an old guy some pleasure," the man said. "God-damn, you nurses are all such prudes."

"It's just that I have a boyfriend," I found myself saying, even though I'd never even kissed a boy. "John Pine," I added for verisimilitude, which was something we were learning about in English class. "Plus, I'm saving myself for marriage."

"Saving yourself for marriage?" he said, shaking his head. "Might as well save your money for the apocalypse."

He closed his eyes as he sucked on his Jell-O. I waited for some sign that I should feed him more. When none came, I put another spoonful in his mouth, though half-mashed pieces from the last bite were still waiting there.

"Sir? Mr."—I glanced at the whiteboard above his head— "Mr. Adams? You have to swallow, or you could choke."

He started snoring loudly. I watched the Jell-O quiver in the darkness of his half-open mouth. I stood there for a minute, and then I spooned the Jell-O from his mouth back into the bowl.

⋆　⋆　⋆

I put off writing my second story, once again, until the evening before it was due. My mother appeared in my doorway, arms crossed. She was dressed in khakis and a white polo, an ensemble required for her shitty, part-time night job, the one she'd tacked on to her schedule after my dad had been laid off. She looked exhausted, her face a little droopy, as if gravity had captured another centimeter of skin.

She pointed at my math book, which was open next to me, asking me why I hadn't started earlier. "Because it's *math*," I said. She gave me the mom look indicating that I had provided the wrong answer. I hadn't even told her about the Write Stuff—as far as she knew, I was still on the crew for the school play.

"Sorry," I said. "But I'm done now! I just finished!" I slammed my math book shut and started getting into my pajamas, which were hanging off the back of my chair.

"Come here," she said softly, and I went to her.

She kissed me on the forehead, her arms still crossed. "Good night," she said, and then she left the room, closing the door behind her.

I heard her walk to the guest room, as she did every night. I pictured her standing in the doorway, arms crossed, the same way she stood in mine. Tonight, instead of just saying good night, I heard her scold my father. "Get out of this bed, and do something—anything," she said. I couldn't hear my dad. Maybe he didn't say anything. "I mean it," she said. "If I don't see you up tomorrow, I'm dragging you out of this house myself."

Then she made a show of clomping down the stairs in her sneakers.

I settled back in my seat. I decided that the man in my story was a narcoleptic with saggy costume-like skin who was so intolerable that his wife tried to poison his soup one night. When he passed out, his frightened daughter called the hospital, though she didn't mention the poison. At the hospital, the narcoleptic suddenly shot up from his gurney and, with a twisted smile, said, "Great! I needed a vacation from my nagging wife!"

I stepped off the bus the next day and saw that my father was outside. It was a biting, windy fall day that had whipped some of the leaves off their branches. As I walked closer, I realized my father had pulled a big square of blue siding off the house and was now pulling off more. The power tools were strewn across the yellowish lawn, and he was covered in dust. He kept stopping to rub his eyes, though his hands were covered in dust too.

I stood behind him, watching him try to rip a nail out of a piece of siding with the claw of a hammer. "Hey," I said. "I guess your headache is gone."

He turned around, leaving the hammer hanging from the nail. His skin was chapped red, and his eyes were wet from the wind.

He rubbed at his eyes again with his dusty hand. "You should go in the house," he said finally. "There's asbestos out here."

"Asbestos? Doesn't that cause cancer?" I asked. "Shouldn't you be wearing, like, a face mask?"

"It's fine. They just have these precautions so they don't get sued."

"Then why can't I stand here? And what are you doing?"

"Just fixing some things," he said. He was back at the nail again.

"So, your headache's gone?"

He turned back toward me. "Go inside," he said again, dust falling from his eyelashes. "I don't want you to get this in your face."

That night, the three of us sat at the dinner table together eating a hamburger macaroni dish we called Tuesday special. My dad pushed his food around, dust falling into his noodles.

"So, I see you've decided to tear the house apart," said my mother. She hadn't said anything about it until then. She'd just walked past him without a word, entered the house, and started making dinner.

But I had noticed, recently, that the space beneath her eyes was growing darker, grayish, like the shadows under the eyes of the troglodytes in corridor D.

"Well, you said—" my father began.

"Getting outside was a good idea," I interrupted, "but maybe you shouldn't be getting into the asbestos."

"Asbestos?" said my mom.

"Just kidding," I said. "I made that up."

"I think I need a nap," said my dad. He left his plate full of food on the table and walked back upstairs.

I ran through the downpour and into the hospital, soaked by the time I got inside. The rain started needling sideways in a way that was kind of exciting, striking the windows so hard and fast that it sounded like an arena broken out in applause.

I tried to dry off in the bathroom under the hand dryer, which didn't really work. The red vest was still sopping, so I stuffed it in one of the volunteer lockers and pinned the VOLUNTEER badge to my slightly less wet shirt. My plan was to head down to medical records for another story idea, but as I turned the corner near mental health, a nurse said, "We could use you in here," motioning toward the forbidden wing.

I hesitated. "Come on," she said, pulling me along.

I'm not sure what I'd expected—maybe I thought some lunatics would be walking around wearing underwear as hats—but the floor didn't look all that different from the others in the hospital. We passed a patient power walking the hall. "This is worse than being a mall walker, isn't it?" he said.

There was, at least, an old, hunchbacked woman slumped in a wheelchair near the nurses' station shouting "I love you!" to everyone who passed, as if her voice were motion activated.

The nurse was rattling off information and looking into rooms as she walked. "It's all hands on deck for a bus accident coming into emergency, so we're pretty short-staffed here," she said. I was sure someone would kick me out, but not a single nurse or doctor even glanced in my direction. "There's a woman in one forty that gets a little hysterical from time to time, but we don't really want to restrain her. Whenever it rains, she thinks the sky is falling."

The nurse stopped suddenly, and I almost ran into her. "Belinda!" she shouted, waving down a nurse across the hall. "Just keep her company, would you?" she said to me, already walking away.

I was overwhelmed by my good fortune.

I peeked into 140 before I entered. The lights were off, and the woman was facing away from me, looking out the window where rain was pounding hard in the parking lot, the trees along the edge twisting back and forth as if they were being tortured for information they didn't have.

"Some weather," I said. I sat on the salmon-colored pleather chair near the bed, the kind of chair all the rooms had.

The woman turned toward me as if in slow motion. Only then did I realize she was crying. She was middle-aged, maybe a few years older than my parents, maybe a decade older. Her off-white nightgown was oversized and pilly. Thick strands of hair were stuck to the sides of her face with sweat or tears or both.

"The rain!" she said, her eyebrows wrinkled in grave concern.

"It's supposed to stop soon," I said, though I hadn't seen a weather report.

"It's pieces of the sky falling down."

"No," I said, and tried to think of some way to prove this while she stared at the ceiling.

"Why are you here?" she asked.

"I thought I'd keep you company."

"They sent you in here, those nurses. To watch me."

"No," I said. "I didn't have anything else to do, so I thought I'd sit here."

"You're lying." She turned her body away from me. "They send a kid!" she added, and then went silent.

I sat in the chair, trying to think of something to say. "Mrs. Peg Michaels" the whiteboard above the bed said with a smiley face next to it. The rain was torrential now, the parking lot just a gray blur outside the window. But the noise was rhythmic, like a meditation soundtrack, and I started to feel peaceful and a little drowsy.

Peg turned toward me so suddenly that I almost jumped. "Listen," she said. "Can you listen to a lady like me?"

"Yes," I said, leaning toward her.

"They won't let me talk to my husband. You have to help me. I just want him to know where I am, so he doesn't worry."

"You aren't allowed to call him?" I asked.

"Do you have a piece of paper? Write this down." I found a little pad and pen in the drawer of the nightstand, and then stood in front of the tray table and began writing down the husband's information, including his address in North Carolina and his phone number. "Will you call him? Please?"

I went straight to the nurses' station, almost running into an orderly on the way, trying to look like I had urgent information while I waited for someone to notice me. The hunchbacked wheelchair lady was still there, and she kept telling me she loved me in a voice so desperate I finally whispered back, "I love you too."

Belinda appeared at the computer and started ticking away at the keys with the tips of her bright pink fingernails, not acknowledging me until she finally said "Yes? Was there something you wanted?" without looking up.

"I was in room one forty—" I began.

"Does she need to be restrained?"

"What? No. It's just, her husband. He doesn't know she's here and—"

"That's because he's dead."

"Dead?"

"He died seventeen years ago."

"But—"

Belinda looked up from the computer with a face that said I was an idiot. "Did she tell you the sky is falling? Did you believe that?"

"But what should I tell her?" I asked.

"I love you!" the woman in the wheelchair suggested.

"Change the subject," said Belinda. "She likes the beach. Her favorite color's red."

Her favorite color—was this lady kidding me? I must have looked annoyed, because Belinda threw one hand in the air as she continued key-pecking with the other. "I don't know," she said. "Tell her that her husband's dead, if you want, but she'll probably take the news as if she's hearing it for the first time."

I walked slowly back to 140, trying to think if I knew anything interesting about beaches.

When I returned, Peg was looking out the window again. Her fingers were white from gripping the metal side rails, as if she were on some horrific amusement park ride. I could see the thick stitches running like train tracks up and down one of her wrists.

"I'm sorry," I said, sinking back into the chair, "that it took so long."

She turned to me, expectant.

"It took a minute, but I got in contact with him. With your husband."

"You're lying!"

"Why would I lie?" I said, feeling strangely confident. "I don't know you. I called him myself. Obviously the nurses were against it, so I wouldn't tell them if I were you."

"What did he say?" she asked, half skeptical, half curious.

"That he misses you very much, that he had wondered where you were and why you hadn't called. I told him you'd been trying. He said that it was okay, as long as you were safe."

"Sure," said Peg, nodding. "He would say that."

"He said he loves you, that North Carolina is warm...but not nearly warm enough without you. He's doing well—he told me to say that. He is really going to be okay, and if you are doing okay or not okay, he still loves you." Peg was smiling now, staring at the ceiling, her grip loosening on the rails. "Can you hear me?" I asked, but she didn't answer.

"He asked that you remember the Carolina sunsets, how beautiful they were, the nights you spent on the beach together, where you shared a red knit cardigan, an arm for each of you. You two stretched the back so thin that after that, it was too big for one person. He still has the cardigan. He keeps it in the drawer where he keeps his pajamas. At night sometimes, when he can't sleep, he takes it out and smells it and thinks of you.

"He has so many memories of you, good ones," I said. "Even the times you were so sad you just lay in bed all day and he didn't know what to do, didn't know how to make you happy, even then he loved you. Even when he told you that you had to change, had to get better, he still loved you, even then. Even when you wouldn't go to work, wouldn't do the chores, he would still take out that cardigan and think of you, of that time on the beach when you were both so happy. Because you *were* happy, once. He couldn't forget that other version of you. He never lost hope."

My eyes felt weighted in their sockets, the way I felt before I might cry. Maybe this woman would never get better. Maybe she would lie around in bed for the rest of her life. Maybe she would never be what her husband wanted her to be.

But of course—I'd already forgotten—her husband was dead.

I blinked myself back to reality, letting Peg come into focus.

She was looking right at me, maybe even through me, to the center of my brain. Her eyes were narrowed and full of hate. "You little bitch," she hissed. I felt my jaw go slack.

She let go of my gaze very slowly, as if to be sure I had understood her, and then turned back toward the window. Outside, the storm was dying down. Light rain pattered in the parking lot over a mosaic of wind-torn leaves. A man in a trench coat jogged toward the hospital with a newspaper splayed over his head. A black umbrella bobbed gently among the parked cars. Beads of rain rolled down the window in thin, glistening tracks.

First Aid

COLOR

My blood comes out a different color every time I slit a new gill. I call them gills because they help me breathe. Every feeling has its own color, and that's the way to know what I'm feeling, cut myself open and see: red, angry; blue, sad; et cetera. Yellow is happiness and it's a great sign when I cut myself open and realize it's been happiness I've been feeling all along.

EXAMPLE

See these here, on the underside of my forearm? It's okay, don't look away, they aren't fresh, they're almost nothing now, just twenty or so raised lines—swoosh, swoosh, swoosh—running parallel to the wrist, my vein a green river running through them.

The newer lines are still pink and hopeful, but the old ones are white as ivory, dead as ghosts.

GRAY

Almost all the tools I use to exude my colors are gray—bleak, cloudy, gray-sky gray—which is the color I feel always unless I allow the others to escape. Here's a lesson from basic psychology. Let's say something bad happens to you. You can't stop the bad thing from happening, because you're too little, or whatever. You roll up into a ball like a gray stone and let the bad thing happen to you. It's an ideal solution, because stones feel nothing. (There's a Simon and Garfunkel song all about this.) But, new problem: How does one become human again after being a stone?

GOOD OLD DAYS

Once upon a time, I had the luxury of using whatever tools were at hand. Still, one had to be secretive. In the high school bathroom, I took a cheap pink plastic razor, the disposable kind you buy in a six-pack, and smashed it apart with the heel of my sneaker so little plastic pieces went pinging all over the beige tiled floors and the blue stall doors. I was trying to get the blade out, but it was, like, glued in there, and I spent almost all of fifth-period Spanish class standing in a stall trying to peel that silver blade out of the pink plastic head, getting my fingers all bloody in the process, which was not the objective, but not a major problem either. I hope these razor manufacturers have won some sort of prize for durable construction. When the blade was finally free (a little mangled with pink chunks still stuck to it), I pushed it into my forearm one, two, ten times, quick slits, just an inch or two long, gaping like mouths shouting or singing, spitting up blood in red and blue. The feelings that had been trapped under my skin whooshed out of me, dripping down my arm, mixing together in a nice, moody dark purple, like a nightshade vegetable.

THINGS PEOPLE HAVE TAKEN AWAY

Razors, knives, and scissors, of course, but also my silver stud earrings in the shape of little skulls, my gray tweezers and my matching nail clippers, my green emery board nail file (but why?), my Tic Tac container of black bobby pins, my brown woven belt with the silver buckle, my pink rabbit's foot, the lime-green shoe-laces from my sneakers, my fluorescent plastic CD cases, even the white points of my fingernails, cut with my own nail clippers into a black plastic trash can under some woman's desk. They have also taken away the cutlery and have replaced it with bendy white plastic utensils. The plastic knife has a useless serrated edge that just mushes into things, leaving indents in the white bread, which looks like a sad cloud and tastes like air.

YELLOW

There is something that feels like an eel when it swims around in my mouth, bony but soft. The boys like this very much, when I let their eels swim around in my mouth. God, do boys exude their own colors at these times! And so liberally too in so many shades of yellow! It's such a beautiful thing, to find people who know exactly how they feel. It'll really wear out the knees of a gal's jeans, especially on those hard-tiled high school bathroom floors.

If there were a boy in front of me right now, I would probably glance down at the ground because I am shy, but if he were in front of me and it was dark, or if I just closed my eyes and let myself float away a little, I would give him whatever he wanted, and I would hope that he would turn electric yellow inside of himself. I would very much hope that whatever insides he wanted outside of himself would come right out.

WHAT DO YOU WANT?

Absurd, but it's the question this guy keeps asking me, over and over, leaning toward me as if he expects me to tell him an important secret, his black desk chair squeaking while I sit across from him on the hard green vinyl upholstery of this ugly wooden chair. "I don't know," I keep saying. There is a whole day outside this guy's window that I don't know anything about except for a tiny blob of cloud and an arthritic branch with a few green leaves fluttering off of it. This guy, he has thick black glasses that are too big for his head and slip down his nose until he manages to push them up at the very last second. He pushes them with his index finger, as if he is mocking nerds. He seems to be cultivating an expression of stern boredom, and while I would be very happy to help him feel a little yellow inside of himself, he doesn't seem amenable. Instead, he wants to know what makes *me* feel a little yellow inside of *myself*. "I don't know, I don't know, I don't know," I keep saying. Jesus Christ, one of us says. Just make up an answer, he tells me. "Cutlery," I say.

CONCENTRATE

I am humming tunes from grade school that I didn't even remember I remembered. I hum softly, and just the thinnest wisp of a note echoes off the tiled floor, the plain walls, returning to my ears so I hear it again:

> People are dying, children are crying.
> Concentrate! Concentrate!
> Let the blood run down.
> Let the blood run down
> and the shivers run up.

We would act out each part, tickling our fingers down each other's backs to show the blood running down, and then wiggling them up for shivers. We were only children, and yet we were singing such awful songs! Who taught them to us? And how were we to know what we were being taught?

RAINBOWS

A rainbow is the gill of the sky. The terrible gray cloudy sadness of a rainy day has been slit right open to reveal the colors that have been hiding under there all along. When the sky is sad, it's because it's so far away from everything that's happening, but it knows exactly what's going on and can't do a thing about it.

FUN! FACT

A rainbow doesn't really have bands; this is a limit of human vision. Likewise, there aren't words for every feeling; this is a limit of human vocabulary. It's difficult to understand things you can neither see nor name.

BLUE

See these slicers, between my fingers? "Taste the rainbow!" the TV in the rec room was exclaiming again and again. I don't know how anyone concentrates with that thing on. I was trying to read a book, a little Dover paperback of Emily Dickinson poems with pages thin as newspaper, the kind where when you touch the words your fingers come away dirty. For every poem I finished reading, I congratulated myself by rubbing the crack between my fingers swiftly along the page's bottom edge as I turned it. Soon the pages I'd turned were wet with sad blue blood, and the ones I hadn't were still dreary and dry, and then I just started to turn the pages—slit, slit, slit!—and the words didn't matter at all.

OTHER THINGS PEOPLE HAVE TAKEN AWAY

The art paper, the books.

OCEAN LIFE

When I can't make gills it's like I'm living underwater but can't really breathe. What I mean is, the picture is hazy and I feel kind of nauseous, like I'm floating around in slow motion, blug blug, like I've been stone-weighted and sunk down to the bottom of something, so I'm half consciously swaying back and forth along the sand with the currents.

People can get pretty angry when they discover I've discovered a new way to gill myself up, but these are the kinds of people that don't need gills to know what they're feeling, and thus they shouldn't have the authority to take something so useful away from those of us who do.

THINGS PEOPLE CANNOT TAKE AWAY

My teeth, edges, corners: nightstand corners, bed corners, wall corners. When I bang up against them, I can see a little bit of color pool there under my skin. Not as satisfying as a gill, but it still helps me breathe.

NO MORE LIES

Life is like singing a few songs over and over that you learned when you were young that you can't stop singing.

This one, for example:

Ask me no more questions
Tell me no more lies
The boys are in the bathrooms
opening their—
Flies are in the meadow,
Bees are in the park
The boys and the girls
are kissing in the
d-a-r-k, d-a-r-k,
dark, dark, dark!

D-A-R-K

Seriously, ask me no more questions. That one's for Mr. Thick Black Glasses, who wants to know all about the dark, dark, dark. Problem: the things that happen in the dark, they're all shades of gray. When I can't see the colors, I don't know what I feel, and when I don't know what I feel, I start to float away. This isn't just about me: every goddamn girl in this place knows the complications that can occur in the d-a-r-k, d-a-r-k, dark, dark, dark.

OCEAN LIFE II

If enough terrible things happen to me, I will turn into an iridescent fish, and I will be thankful for it. It will be better than being human, because I'll be silver-gray as well as every other shining, shimmering color. And I'll have gills! I'll be very slippery, yes, but also soft and very quick. My brain will be tiny and I'll act by instinct alone.

RED

This one on my thigh? As you can see, it has been stitched up, and that feeling was stitched right back up inside of me, like a pillow pressing up against my face so I can't breathe. I did it with a paper clip I found in the hallway. It had shone up at me from the tiled floor with a dot of light like the glint in someone's eye. *Aha!* I thought. I bent at the waist as if I was touching my toes, but I picked up that paper clip instead, feeling the cool, curved metal between my forefinger and thumb. Later, in the d-a-r-k, dark, dark, dark, I unbent the paper clip and pressed the sharp tip hard against my inner thigh. Oh that feeling! There is nothing that can compare to letting your insides outside of you! Even in the night, I could sense that the color of my blood was bright red, like a fresh tomato on a very green farm. How could I have known how angry I was until I saw it for myself? My anger felt healthy, meditative. I pulled the gill apart, pressing my fingers into the open cut, letting the warm sting of pain flow through me.

CREATIVE VISION

Imagine this: a rainbow of cuts on my forearm, the arching gills curving at my wrist, each one dripping a different color, the colors cascading into one another, rolling down my arm, pooling in the elbow-bend nook of my arm, and then spilling over the edges, as when tears fall into your ears as you lie in bed crying. Except when the tears fall into your ears, they feel foreign, they feel like someone else's tears. These tears will feel like they're mine.

What will happen next? It's hard to say, but I think perhaps all of these gills will unite in a chorus of song. The song will be so magnificent and arresting that it will replace the memories of all of the songs I have ever heard sung, and it will be the new song I will hum to myself for the rest of my life.

FIRST AID

I know people think I'm crazy, but I don't care. I've saved myself hundreds of times just like this. And let me ask you: how many times have you saved yourself with just a few basic cuts?

Human bonding

It was the semester I snorted coke off a toilet, smoked weed in an alley with a homeless guy named Caesar, and was black-eyed by some girl on the street at 2 a.m., somebody's girlfriend. It was the semester I tripped up the splintering steps of my apartment complex and lay there in my own drool/vomit until morning, when a neighbor stepped on my hand, a story that wouldn't be worth telling except that the sole of his shoe said SUSEJ, so that he could leave Jesus prints in the sand or wherever he was, like on my hand, where he left one in a diagonal, purple bruise. When I saw him later in the hall I made sure my hand faced forward so he could see what he'd done, but he just looked down at it with a stony expression and then back into my eyes, one of which was greenish purple and as big as an egg. I figured he viewed the Jesus print as some kind of sign from God, and maybe it was.

"Sorry," I said because I was in his way, though I didn't move to get out of it.

"You're a girl?" he asked, surprised, because I have this pompadour hair and a James Dean wardrobe, but my voice is unmistakable. He looked at me for a minute like I was a puppy he'd discovered in a garbage can.

It was also my last semester because I stopped going to the class I needed in order to graduate, and I didn't feel like retaking it. But before all of that, it was the semester I met Wendy.

I first saw her in a crowded lecture hall, her golden curls shining from the sea of dull hair, a thin strip of pure white light hitting her head so that it looked like she was wearing a headband. Her dress bloomed with violets. I sat down next to her, blocking the sun, and looked over her arm at the bubbly, printed words at the top of the first page of a new notebook, the date and the day's topic ("Introduction"). Each letter was so defined, so singular, it seemed as if it had its own personality. Seeing them, I felt like a child with my face pressed up against the cool glass of a high-rise city window watching a bright, happy parade go by.

The class, which fulfilled some distribution requirement everyone else had apparently knocked off freshman year, met at an unfortunate 9:00 a.m., MWF.

"This is Human Bonding," the professor said, extending two hands out over the lectern as if we ourselves were the topic of the class, "but if you came here thinking this class was about sex, then you were more than half mistaken."

This was only my first more-than-half mistake. My second was asking Wendy to lend me a pen, or maybe that was my third, and my second was sitting next to her in the first place. When I asked to borrow a pen, Wendy, whose name I had yet to learn, nodded without a word, which surprised me. I had expected that squint-eyed scrutiny you often get from the kind of girl who writes down the date in her notebook—like the kind of person who's forgotten a pen is also the kind of person who won't return it. Wendy leaned over her backpack and pulled out a pencil case featuring Hello Kitty's disembodied and mouthless head. She extracted four pens and laid them out on my desk, each one a different color.

"I'm not ambi-ambidextrous," I said, and she laughed even though the joke was dumb.

"I thought you might have a preference," she said. A preference! In pen color! I chose the pink one, and watched to see if this would tickle her, and it did, I could tell by her smile. Her smile was wide and forgiving, with deep dimples, but when she started taking notes, her mouth became small and her lips jutted out in a gently pouting kiss.

I copied the date and topic from her notebook on a crumpled piece of paper I'd found in my pocket. I wrote my name at the top, as an afterthought, "CHRIS," in all caps, as if it mattered if I lost this piece of paper, as if someone could somehow return it to me if I did. Taking notes was a particularly fruitless endeavor—my penmanship was terrible; even I could hardly decipher it. In the whole mess of moving in with my grandparents after my mom passed, I missed the unit on cursive, and now I was too lazy to either learn it or pick up my pen between letters, so my handwriting looked like the EKG squiggle of someone near death.

Wendy had already written down four or five lines of notes, bullet-pointed, including things I already knew wouldn't be a problem for her ("Late homework = ZERO"). I didn't feel like copying them, I just watched her arm as it moved back and forth so diligently across the page. That arm was pale white, almost glowing, like a star.

That semester, I woke up in many different beds and in many different conditions, but I would always arrive at class MWF relatively on time. Headached and hungover as I often was, I liked having a destination other than my stuffy apartment, which had no furniture save an air bed and a microwave and made me feel like a squatter in my own life. Wendy was already in class, always, settled into her seat completely, notebook page dated, pens spread across my little beige flip-up desk for the choosing. She was my tour guide through the syllabus ("Short answers due Wednesday," she'd remind me as we filed out of the lecture hall), my summarizer of readings. Hers was the notebook I'd look to after I'd accidentally fallen asleep or gotten lost in a daydream.

Wendy was different from the women I usually woke up next to. She was fresh and balanced—not chipper per se, but she seemed like she slept eight hours each night and had milk and cereal for breakfast with slices of banana cut on top.

One morning, her dress looked like a garden, and the blue and purple flowers seemed to spring from her very flesh. After my usual *hmm*ing bit over which pen to choose, I asked Wendy how old she was. Class hadn't started yet and students were still shuffling in around us. I don't even know why I asked—I already knew she was a freshman. I had this weird half idea that she might be one of those kids who skipped high school and went straight to college.

She was eighteen, as she should have been. "Is it because of this?" she asked, holding up her pink pencil case and looking concerned. Hello Kitty stared at me with that expressionless face, just two black oval eyes that you could pretend meant anything you wanted.

"No," I said, waving it away, but that wasn't entirely true. Of course it wasn't *just* the pencil case; it was the whole thing, her ambiance, the floral dresses and the dimples and the way she smiled. I knew things just by looking at her, the way, when people saw me, they knew instantly that I was a fuckup.

I wanted to tell Wendy that she should like what she liked, that not pretending to be the same as everyone else was what made her more interesting than these people all around us. Case in point were two girls a row in front of us with orange-brown spray tans and hair solidified with so much product that it practically clinked as they turned their heads, which they often did at the same exact moment.

But I didn't elaborate because I knew where compliments could lead, and it wasn't a place I wanted Wendy to go, not with me, at least. I clasped my hands together like my mother used to tell me to do when I was little, when I couldn't seem to prevent myself from getting into trouble.

When I picture my mom, I picture her above me, a shadow, hovering or holding me, scolding or comforting me after I'd done something wrong. A golden cross always rested on the flat plain above her breasts. That cross often swung above my head like a pendulum as my mother leaned over me, or was clutched in my fist, the tall point rising between my fingers, warm from her chest and surprisingly sturdy for something so thin.

My mother, so kind and patient, and still I had discarded every-thing she had ever given me, my name and the lessons she had taught me, how to sew and sift flour, how to braid my own hair and say the Lord's Prayer: *And lead us not into temptation . . .*

I was buzzed on tequila, standing outside a bar off College Ave that had once let me in with a fake ID identifying me as a race I am not with a color hair I don't have. It was newly dark and a little cool, and I was smashing a cigarette under the toe of my sneaker, feel-ing smugly proud of myself—that I'd more or less shown restraint: a few shots of tequila, one cigarette, still relatively early, time to go home—when Wendy walked by, looking down at something in her hands, not noticing me, the skirt of her dress flowing along below her purple backpack like flowers in the wind.

"Hey," I yelled. She stopped, turned, waved, walked back to me. The moon was as round as a quarter, and under it Wendy's curls glistened. "Your hair looks nice," I said. She smiled down at the ground as I moved my foot forward to cover the cigarette. "You at the library?" I asked. "Until now?"

"Flash cards," she said, holding up a stack of colored index cards. I squinted in hopes of making out that bubbly handwriting I liked so much, but all I could see was a blur. I counted in my head how much I'd drunk, little shot glasses floating over a fence like sheep: one, two, three, et cetera—it was hard to say, but it seemed like they'd all caught up with me.

"What are they for?" I asked.

"Our class," she said. I stared at her dumbly, and her face went serious. "For the test tomorrow. I told you."

"Shit," I said before I could stop myself. I tried to remember whether or not we'd reviewed the syllabus together that week. "Can we go through them?"

"Now?" she asked.

"Yeah," I said, and you could say I didn't know what I was doing, but I am often both stupider and not as stupid as I seem.

Wendy looked down at her flash cards and then up at me, as if she had to choose between us. I tried to stand steady. "All right," she said. "All right, yes. I live right over here."

She lived a few blocks from the bar. We walked up a dark stairwell where peeling paint revealed layers of rejected colors all the way down to fifties mint green. The wooden stairs were creaky, like some animal was under there moaning in pain every time we took a step.

"Why doesn't someone get these stairs fixed?" I asked.

"They're just creaky," said Wendy. But this wasn't the kind of place Wendy was supposed to be living in, with stairs you could probably fall through into an apartment below, some drug dealer's lair for all anyone knew.

Her apartment, a studio, was much nicer than the stairway, and I knocked on the wall as if from this action I could decipher something about structural soundness. A rickety-looking round table was covered in opened textbooks, stray papers, a mess of pens, a plate covered in crumbs and deflated grapes. Her beige linoleum kitchen was stacked with precarious towers of dirty plates, bowls, and mugs. Several posters, including van Gogh's sunflowers, were tacked right into the wall with red and blue pushpins.

The main event of the room, though, was perfectly organized

and, I thought, the best representation of Wendy herself: a futon folded out into a bed with a multicolored floral comforter and two matching pillows, a collection of stuffed animals nestled between and in front of them, arranged by height, with the smallest, not more than five inches high, sitting at the very front. They were all staring off into space with hard black plastic eyes and soft threaded smiles.

I sat on the floor across from Wendy, running my finger up and around the knots in the wood, trying not to look at her. But even from that position I could still see her knees tucked under her, white and smooth, the snowy peaks of two mountains. I watched her delicate fingers pick a word from the tall rainbow of flash cards, listened to her soft voice as she read aloud. The cards were all about how a baby attaches to its mother, how that's some kind of template for the future, like if you don't give a shit if your mother leaves you alone in a playroom when you're two you're fucked for life, and you'll never give a shit when anyone leaves you in the future. As if life could be boiled down to one variable.

I didn't want to look up at Wendy's face because I knew what that would come to, and even as I didn't look at her face, I knew that I was simply delaying the inevitable. I knew a lot of things about the future. I knew that I should leave, for example, but I also knew that I wouldn't, not unless Wendy asked me to, and in a way I hoped she would.

"Hey, you okay?" Wendy asked, tapping me on the knee.

I looked up at her and nodded. Her curls, her pink cheeks, her pink lips: a porcelain doll. Something flashed through my mind, something my mom had always said, that I was like a bull in a china shop. *Don't touch now, baby,* echoed through my head.

But I always did.

I swirled my pointer finger down the length of one of Wendy's curls. She put her fingers around her flash cards, realigning them. I saw her lips turn up in a little smile that she wanted to keep to herself. I put my finger under her chin. She was warm, pulsing with energy, like a child or a star, but she didn't move. I kissed her. "I shouldn't do this," I said, but my hand was already working through the buttons in the rosebush of her dress. My hand was shaking. "You shouldn't let me do this." Her chest was blinding white. I closed my eyes. I didn't want to see. It was like undressing a doll. I was vibrating, my whole body. She put her hands under my shirt, spreading her fingers out over my bare back and down my sides like a waterfall. I kissed her neck. She was right there, under my tongue: Wendy.

Wendy led me to the bed. It unnerved me a little, how naturally she did this. I took off my clothes, even though I was feeling self-conscious, which was weird, because I'd done this a million times, even with girls who were kind of gross, girls with missing front teeth and meth problems and BO. She pushed all of the stuffed animals off the bed in one giant sweep, then lay on her back. With the stuffed animals all sprawled across the floor, the whole place was a disaster.

I started kissing her, working my way down, but nothing felt right, nothing felt natural. The stuffed animals that had landed faceup—teddy bears and monkeys and a goddamn pink caterpillar—were all staring at me. Their mouths were spread into thin, knowing smiles, like they had been taught the facts of life a long time ago. They had eyes like the Mona Lisa.

I wanted to leave. I heard Wendy saying, "Hey, hey," in a voice like a mother patting her crying baby on the back. "Don't worry about me," she said. I figured one of us better finish fast, so I abandoned the task of getting Wendy off and just went at it for my own pleasure.

When I was done, I peeled my sweaty body off her and began collecting my clothes from the floor. I couldn't look at her. "I have to go," I said, jamming my arm through the hole of my T-shirt and flipping it over my head. The radiators were making violent, hammering sounds now, like the moaning creature under the stairs had clambered up through the pipes and was trying to get in. It had gotten hot, so hot it was hard to breathe. "Sorry," I added.

Wendy looked down over the edge of the bed, and I was afraid of the expression I'd see when she turned back toward me: dimpleless cheeks, jutting lip, eyebrows bent up in sorrow, all because I was an asshole.

But when Wendy turned back toward me, her face was dimpleless, yes, but not pained either, not even stoically expressionless. It was just a face completing a task, which had been to grab her underwear from over the side of the bed and slither back into them. She was composed, but not overly or showily. It was like she had expected me to be awful, and she didn't even care.

I slipped my sneakers on without untying them, the backs bent under my heels. "I have to go," I said again, dumbly.

"One sec," she said, and she pulled at the sheet from under the wrinkled comforter, to untuck it from the bottom of the bed, then stood up and wrapped herself in it, and for the first time, in the dim light of the messy room, she could have been any other girl on campus and it made my fucking heart want to crawl into some safer location.

She followed me as I shuffled to the door in my sneakers. "Test at nine, remember?" she said, as if we were just parting ways at the lecture hall.

As soon as she closed the door, I sprinted down the moaning stairs, my toes clawing into the fronts of my sneakers so they wouldn't come off. I started walking up the dark sidewalk, chilly because I hadn't brought a jacket. I fished around in my jeans pockets for some pharmaceuticals. That would have been another good reason to have brought my jacket: more pockets. I took whatever I found without even looking, chewing the stuff, letting the bitter taste spread out across my tongue.

I stopped back at the bar, where I'd begun the night hours before, and had a few shots. I felt far-off again, the way I liked it, myself once removed, like I was controlling a character in a first-person video game. The bar was a dive, all dark wood lacquered in years of beer spills, so the tables and seats were always sticky, and it seemed like no one was ever in there but regulars until it was late, and then wasted college kids came in, like this gaggle of girls in blue-sequined shirts piling in, probably from some themed party. Even in the low light of the bar, their shirts sparkled across the walls like disco balls. Two of the girls were a couple, one of them with big eyes and jet-black hair, the other plain and stiff. They made out in the corner while some townie at the bar cheered them on.

A little later, Big Eyes sidled up next to me to order a beer, and I wrapped my hands around her waist and flung her out into the open space of the bar and started dancing and she giggled and said, "What are you even doing?" I put my cheek to her cheek, the way they dance in old movies, and maybe I tried to kiss her. Then I left.

As soon as I stepped back out into the night, the door hardly out of my hand, I felt a hard tap on my shoulder, and almost by the time I turned around, or at least by the time my vision caught up with the turn, I had already been punched in the eye, a knuckle-cracking whammy followed by a tirade I didn't try to decipher and probably couldn't have because I was too fucked up. My vision tunneled into a pinpoint of black and then expanded out again.

I stumbled backward against the brick wall and then sank down to sit on the sidewalk. The upper-left quadrant of my face ached with heat. I seemed to have been holding my breath, and I let it out all in one puff.

The gaggle of girls gathered in a shimmering blue cloud to try to talk down Big Eyes's girlfriend, who wanted to punch me again. I tried to wink at Big Eyes, but my left eye wouldn't open. Out here in the dark, her eyes were less big. In fact, her whole face seemed different, uglier. People never really were who you wished them to be, were they?

The girls floated down the sidewalk together, glancing back at me with pitying half smiles. For a while, I could still hear their voices echoing into the night, and then it was silent save the low buzz of buildings. I lay down on the cold sidewalk and closed the eye that still worked, smiling to myself. I'd never been punched in the face before, believe it or not. It felt good, it felt like justice.

THE WAYSIDE

"It's not just the words, it's the attitude: the excitement you bring to the house and the people who lived here. You have to start animated *and* you have to keep that energy going the whole way through. For example—" He paused for a moment, his finger on his lips, and then put on his tour guide face: eyes wide, mouth stretched into an impossible smile. "Welcome to the Wayside. I'm your tour guide, James." I thought the smile might pop off his face. "The tour should take approximately one half hour, *and* I'll be available to answer any questions you have up to a half hour after the tour is over."

He paused and relaxed, still smiling. "Sort of like that," he said. "I'm sure you've got it, May. You catch on fast."

"Yeah, you keep saying I've got it, *but* you haven't let me do a tour yet," I said, brushing my hair back with my hand for the millionth time that day. It was the summer between my senior year of high school and my freshman year of college, a humid

New England summer that made my hair puff out so that I was constantly pinning or brushing it back despite the low success rate of such tactics.

"You're almost ready," he said, "*and* I think you only need a few more tours before we give you a run."

"*But,*" I said, "I can do it after that?"

We had a war going on between "and"s and "but"s, or, at least, I had a war going on between "and"s and "but"s. James believed "but" was a negative word that subtracted positive meaning from the first part of the sentence, and therefore he rarely used it. He would say things like, "You're doing a great job entering data into the computer *and* when you file my papers I can't seem to find them."

To counter his irrational elimination of "but," I used it as frequently as possible in places where it was completely unnecessary: "I really like oranges," I'd say during lunch break, "*but* I really like apples." I'd never dared to play such a game with my teachers, and maybe I only had the courage to play it now because I knew he wouldn't get angry—his smile rarely disappeared, as if a parenthesis had been tattooed below his nose.

This was the first time I'd been employed as anything besides a babysitter, and I was unprepared for such thorough and personal training. By the end of my first week, I felt as if I'd been at the Wayside for half the summer. I arrived at work each morning preemptively exhausted to find James smiling absurdly, eager to start. His mouth was frog-like: broad and slightly protruding, his lips long, thin, and pink. I wondered which came first, his smile or the shape of his mouth. He was lean and clean-shaven, wore thin silver-rimmed spectacles that nearly matched his silvering hair. I imagined that each morning, after sit-ups and egg whites, he stood barefoot on a white-tiled bathroom floor, shaving carefully, a pile of lather falling into an impossibly white sink.

What I'd really wanted was a job at the Orchard, the historic site next door, where Louisa May Alcott had written *Little Women* and also where my best friend, Julie, worked. The Wayside and the Orchard couldn't have been more different. The Wayside *seemed* charming from the outside: a creamy house with green shutters, a wraparound porch, and an extra room that jutted from the roof alongside three pink chimneys. The Orchard was just a big box with long dark brown siding in the typical old–New England fashion.

But inside, the Orchard was bright and cheery, as if the little women could come tumbling down the stairs at any moment. The Wayside, on the other hand, was so dreary inside it looked like a set for a murder mystery. It was cold, even in the summer, with bile green carpets and drawn shades that made every day seem overcast and dull. The Wayside's star was Nathaniel Hawthorne, though it had also housed two other notable writers—children's author Margaret Sidney and Louisa May Alcott herself. Famous people had been all over the property, and it was briefly a stop on the Underground Railroad.

On my first Friday at work, James and I waited around to see if anyone would arrive at the visitors' center for the final tour of the week. Or *he* waited for another tour, and I waited for the end of the day. The visitors' center was a small building located thirty feet from the Wayside. Here books were sold, tours began, and life-size plaster statues of each author stood silently before displays of old pictures and famous quotes.

James finished sweeping, leaned his broom against the wall, and then sat in a chair beside me. "What are your aspirations?" he asked. I almost laughed.

"I don't know," I said.

"Writing?" he asked, nodding toward the plaster authors.

"Oh, no," I said. "Not writing." I sensed disappointment, though it's hard to say why since he was wearing his usual smile.

"You can do anything at your age," he said, "and I still believe I can do anything at mine. It's all a matter of enough time, *and* you have yet to worry about that."

But I did, in a way, have to worry about that. I was seventeen—not exactly a child, but not quite an adult. The summer felt like a strange no-man's-land, and I was trying my best not to consider the before and after that so conspicuously surrounded me.

Just then, a girl and her mother entered the visitors' center. "Well, hello!" James said, jumping up as I mustered what I could of a smile.

James stared at the girl for a moment. She was carrying a notebook and pen. He closed his eyes and hummed. The girl watched to see what would happen next. The mother smiled. James opened his eyes, his smile rubber-banding tight across his face. "It just came to me," he said. "I have this feeling...this feeling that you must be...you must be a writer!" He paused. "Am I right?"

The girl giggled and looked at her mother, who motioned for her to respond. "I *am* a writer," said the girl. "And and and"—she again looked up at her mother, who encouraged her to go on—"*and!* I've wrote a story and it was in the...in the *newspaper!*" She said "newspaper" in a whisper, as if it were a secret. James shook his head in amazement. "Wow!" he said. "And how old are you?"

"*Eight* years old!" the girl shouted, and I felt a pang of regret for already being too old to be a child prodigy.

"Well, we'll need to give you a very special tour of the Wayside," said James. It took a very special person to give a special tour of the Wayside—it took a very special person to make the Wayside interesting at all, especially with the cheery Orchard mocking us from next door.

That night, like every Friday night, I had dinner at my dad's tiny apartment in Carlisle, which was just outside Concord. It was barely three rooms: a small kitchen attached to a bedroom attached to a bathroom. Instead of doors, the rooms were separated by hanging wooden beads. The place was neat and sparse: no wall decorations, few shelves, an air mattress for a bed. Extra items were kept in piles: cereal boxes here, gray custodial shirts there. He had found a round table on the street and this was where we spent most of our time, sitting in chairs that were missing bars at the back.

My mom referred to the evenings at my father's as the Weekly Styrofoam Dinners, since we always ordered takeout. After my first week of work, I sat with my legs curled beneath me and my elbows on the table, eating Chinese food from a black plastic box with a black plastic fork. My dad sat across from me, leaning forward to assess the contents of his box. "How's work?" he asked.

"Well," I said, "the guy who runs the place is..." I paused. "He's very nice."

"*Too* nice, you mean," said my dad, poking through his meal.

"Here," I said, pointing with my fork to a shrimp in my dish. "Yeah, too nice, I guess."

"Maybe he wants in your pants." My dad took the shrimp with his fork. He always believed one person was after what was in another person's pants, probably a projection of his own wishes and, I guessed, the reason my parents had split up.

"He's over fifty," I said.

"A young girl like you? He'd love it. Watch out."

I arrived at my mom's later that evening to find the spot where I usually sat at the kitchen table covered in college forms, pages and pages requiring the same exact information. One of the forms was a housing survey. I was supposed to specify if I was a night owl or an early bird. Everything on the survey was a kind of stupid metaphor like that, and I hadn't filled it out yet.

"What are these for?" I asked my mother, who was in the kitchen making her own dinner.

"What are these for?" my mother repeated. "Maybe they're for you to fill out before they're due? What do you think?"

"Well, you're in a good mood," I said, dropping my purse on the floor and heading into the family room to sit on the couch.

"I hope you aren't planning to go off gallivanting with Julie tonight, because you've got plans, honey." Had she been like this when my brother, Frank, was leaving? I couldn't remember.

She walked into the family room, sat on the other side of

the couch, and flipped on the news. I already didn't want to hear it. It always started straightaway with the wars: this person captured, another person killed, trucks blowing up, buildings instantly in smithereens. No mention of Afghanistan—we'd already forgotten about that war but hadn't yet remembered to mention we forgot.

"Do you *have* to watch that?" I asked.

"*I* need to know if my son is safe," she said. Frank was in Afghanistan. I wanted to tell her that her *son* was my *brother* and the news wasn't going to tell her if Frank was okay; all it was going to do was set her on edge and make her worry.

"Have we heard from him?" I asked.

"That email last week," she said, waving me away. "I would've told you."

Frank had gone right from college to the Middle East and had barely returned since, going on new tours every chance he got. I guess he liked war, though it wasn't the kind of thing you wanted to shout from the rooftops in a city like this, even though Bostonians, of all people, were raised with almost a parental love for America, believing that we had been present for both the country's conception and its birth. We loved the revolution, the Constitution, war, peace, and transcendentalism. Every April, Lexington and Concord shut down for Patriots' Day, our own version of Independence Day, marking the first battle of the Revolutionary War with fireworks, barbecues, and beer. Neighbors who I'd only ever witnessed walking lazily down their driveways in button-downs and khakis on that day in April would march in the street carrying giant flags or fake rifles, wearing white wigs and fancy blue or red coats with golden buttons.

But recently, the fireworks had not been as bright or as high or as many. This year, Patriots' Day came just a month after fifty thousand people had gathered in the heart of the city waving poster boards and painted sheets, yelling, "Not one more day! Not one more dollar! Not one more death!" And "How many lives per gallon?" The equation made my stomach churn. I pictured whole lines of soldiers hugging their families goodbye and then, suddenly, in the very arms of a sister or a parent or a wife, each soldier would melt down into a black puddle shining at their feet.

Women would stand behind me in grocery lines saying things like, "Who in his right mind would fight such a useless war?" and "I wouldn't want my son dying over there for no reason." For a while, I couldn't step into a single crowded place without hearing something like that. They claimed to protest on my brother's behalf, and in the next breath they essentially called him an idiot. Sometimes it made me wish I lived in some other city, the apathetic kind they always talked about on the news.

I told him once that he shouldn't have to go. "I don't *have* to go," he said. "We have a *volunteer* army." I wanted to say that he hadn't *volunteered* to be unable to afford college unless he joined the military, but it wasn't the time to get into it. "I *want* to go," he said. "What else am I supposed to do? Go home?" I guess it was one war or the other, but I thought the whole rule in the army was that you didn't leave anybody behind. And Frank had no excuses. He had known what it was like on Evergreen Drive, where, when he'd left, I was stuck alone without him.

When we were little, Frank would invite me into his room when our parents were arguing. Frank's baby blue room was covered with car posters and dusty model airplanes. He'd play music from his lime-green boom box, showing me each tape's case before playing it, pointing to the white sticker where he'd written the album name and artist in careful, black print. "If someone wants to know if these guys are cool, what do you say?" he'd ask. As it turned out, Frank only owned things that were "okay," "cool," or "very cool," so I had three chances.

"You're an idiot," he'd say when I got it wrong, and he'd turn back to the boom box and not look at me until I got it right, at which time he'd look back in my direction and smile, throwing two thumbs up right next to his ears. At those times there was not a sound that existed outside that room.

Between tapes, we'd both shut up and listen. If there was silence, if the argument was over, our game was too, and he'd rub his hand hard into the top of my head. "Get out of here," he'd say, pushing me out the door.

He got all the looks: sandy hair, pink cheeks, a square jaw that I also inherited, though it looked strong and confident on him and out of place on me. Anyway, it was a face you could feel all right about being related to, a face you could end up missing if it wasn't around for you to see it anymore.

Julie visited me on lunch breaks to get a look at the other employees, like Ted. Ted was a graduate student in museum studies completing a practicum at the Wayside. His task, as far as I understood it, was to research the pre-1800s history of the property and write up text for a special installation.

"Hey," Julie would say to him whenever he passed, and he would smile in our direction.

One day, not looking at me, zipping her thumb back and forth across a copy of *The Scarlet Letter* as if it were a flip-book, probably ruining that edge for good, she said, "You wouldn't understand since you have, like, *zero hormones*, but I'm telling you FYI that Ted is cute, should you ever be quizzed on the subject."

"Duh," I said. Julie mistook a lack of experience for a lack of interest. I'd only kissed one person—twice—and when I'd recapped with Julie later I'd said, "It was fine, I guess." She'd laughed until she couldn't breathe.

Ted was thin but not lanky like most of the guys I knew from high school. He had dark brown eyes and an easy confidence. But there was something else: it was as if his face had completely and definitively grown into his face, whereas ours still hadn't quite decided what to be.

Julie and I spent an inordinate amount of time guessing his age. Every time he said something like "When I was in college...," our ears perked up. We cataloged the references he made to movies, important events, and previous jobs, but we avoided making such references ourselves. In his presence, we never talked about our impending college careers or our recent high school graduation, thinking he might like us more if he imagined we were older. Eventually, we pinned him between thirty-two and thirty-six, nixing thirty-seven mostly because it seemed too old. As Julie put it, "Practically forty? Just...no."

If Ted wasn't there, Julie would settle for picking on Audrey. Audrey took James's place at the Wayside twice a week. She was twenty-seven, but her mean-librarian demeanor made her seem older. For lunch, she ate pickles on Hawthorne's front lawn, directly from a jar wrapped in a brown paper bag. She would hold the first pickle lightly between her thumb and forefinger, biting it with a delicate crack, but by the end the bites were ravenous, like she was a monkey chomping at a banana. Pickle juice flew everywhere, so that for the rest of the day she smelled of vinegar. One day, as I was watching her do this, she looked up at me and hissed, "No, I'm not pregnant. I'm trying to lose weight."

Audrey was top-heavy, with a large balloon of a chest and a wide stomach, twiggy legs, and curveless hips. In the end, though, she was about as not-skinny as I was not-skinny, which was not not-skinny enough to require a pickle-only diet.

"She looks like a dog guarding the house," whispered Julie one day, her forearms resting on the counter so that the silver bracelets she usually wore leaned sideways on the back of her hand. "Just like a dog, the way she eats pickles on the grass like that and snarls at me."

"Snarls at you?"

"She obviously doesn't like me," said Julie. Julie had just gotten a French manicure, and her fingers suddenly seemed absurdly long and incredibly clean. "She's so stuck up about her knowledge of *Nathaniel Hawthorne* and everything else. I bet she wants to go to grad school at *Harvard*." She tried to say "Nathaniel Hawthorne" and "Harvard" with a British accent, which she felt to be a signifier of pretentiousness, but they came out more with long Boston *As*.

Audrey didn't quite *snarl*, but she certainly did scowl. She'd gone to Dartmouth and railed on her high school classmates who'd gone to Harvard and were never able to "experience leaving home." But she was twenty-seven and worked at the Wayside, which was in Concord, which was about as close to not leaving home as Audrey could get. We had a lot of Harvard shirts at the Wayside, and Audrey looked at them with contempt. She fared better with those from Boston College, Emerson, or Tufts. I was planning to go to an even lesser known Boston college—not a place of intelligence or stupidity, just a place that offered some money, a resting ground before real life could take hold. And the Wayside? The Wayside was just a rest stop before a rest stop.

"Sorry you got stuck at Wayside," Julie said, scrunching her nose. "Orchard is really fun." Come fall, Julie would be going to college in Manhattan, which was one reason why I'd wanted to work with her this summer.

"James is going to let me do the tours soon," I said, though I wasn't entirely sure this was true.

"He came on my tour on, like, Friday," said Julie.

"At Orchard?"

"I didn't tell you? I heard he visits all the Emerson and Thoreau spots too. He wants to be a writer—he's trying to soak it all in. His smile is so annoying. Like, dude, get ahold of yourself. Life is *not* that exciting."

"It's like he popped out of an after-school special," I said.

Julie laughed as Audrey appeared in the doorway. "Julie," Audrey said in her pissed off way, "you better get back to Orchard."

"You have pickle juice on your skirt, Audrey," said Julie.

I wished Julie wouldn't say things like that, only because Audrey then liked me less and treated me worse, and I had to try to make up for it. But it was true, the pickle juice had dripped into the white script of the A that rested in the bottom corner of her skirt, shading it green. Audrey loved *The Scarlet Letter*. "Wouldn't it be wonderful," she said once, "to be that kind of honorable outcast?" Her wardrobe suggested that when the initialed monogram paraphernalia was having a moment she had purchased all of the A-labeled apparel she could find.

Audrey began organizing the already perfectly organized Hawthorne books on the shelf next to the cash register. "I mean, I like pickles too," I said. Or anyway, I didn't *not* like them.

She grunted.

"So," I said. "You're planning to stay in...the tourism field?"

Audrey turned around. "I'm going into journalism," she said. It was starting to feel like everyone around here was a writer or was trying to be one, as if greatness could rub off on people and onto things and back onto people again.

"What'd you major in during college?" I asked.

"Media studies," said Audrey, who had returned to her organization of books after a pointed look at me. "I minored in English literature, which is only one reason why I work here."

"I don't know what I'll major in," I said. "I'm mostly working here because Julie—"

"Of course," said Audrey.

"Well, I needed a summer job, Audrey."

"Why didn't you go work at the mall or something? Have you even read Hawthorne?"

"In high school," I said. I had. Sort of. I'd read *Little Women* upwards of five times as a kid, but I'd barely managed to get through *The Scarlet Letter* once in my sophomore year. All I could remember was that the first chapter was long and boring and about a door. When I'd started working—after I'd already read all of the captions and quotes on the displays and spent far too many hours tapping out "Hot Cross Buns" on the cash register keys— I'd picked up a copy of *The Scarlet Letter*. The first chapter was only two pages long. It was still boring, as far as I could tell, and it was still, more or less, about a door.

"Anyway, it doesn't matter," I said. "Is this what you did before college? Work here?"

Audrey turned toward me again. "Look," she said, almost nicely, "it's not like I've been working here for my whole life. College is a big thing. You change. Watch it. You'll see. You won't want to work here next summer."

"Besides," she added, "you'll probably go into something like retail management." She was at the books again, running a finger delicately across a long, even row of *The Scarlet Letter*.

One morning I came upon James just as he was opening the visitors' center. It was already humid, but James had a smile on his face and a song in his heart. "You're whistling, this early?" I asked.

He stopped whistling. "I'm at my favorite job," he said.

"Are you ever *not* happy?" I hadn't eaten breakfast yet. My hair was frizzed out in the sun.

"Sometimes, *and* even sadness gives us a larger view of life." It was too much at this hour. I was glad I hadn't eaten breakfast—nothing to puke up. He started whistling again, entered the visitors' center, and began dusting Louisa May Alcott.

"*And,*" he said without looking up, "you can do the first tour today."

"Really? *But* do you think I'm ready?" I was nervous.

"Just one for today, *and* you can do more as the summer goes on."

I spent the morning cleaning Hawthorne down to his nostrils, tapping out quick versions of "Mary Had a Little Lamb" on the cash register keys, realigning the spines of books, repeating facts over and over. The dates were the hardest to remember. "Nathaniel Hawthorne, born 1804," I whispered. "Louisa May Alcott, 1832. Margaret Sidney, 1844." At ten to noon, a family of four entered the visitors' center.

"Welcome to the Wayside!" I shouted, and they all jumped like I was one of the statues come to life. "Would you like a tour?" I asked. "I'm your tour guide, May."

"Um, yes," the father mumbled. "A tour."

"It will begin in ten minutes," I said, trying to quell my nerves. The little boy started throwing fake punches at Nathaniel Hawthorne's creamy white leg, and the little girl tugged on her mother's dress, asking when they were getting ice cream.

I did about as well on my first tour as I should have expected. As we walked up the steep steps to the highest point in the house, the Sky Parlor, as Hawthorne had called it, the mother complained, "But none of this is even Hawthorne's furniture?" James trailed behind us, watching how I fared.

"Well, it's Margaret Sidney's stuff. She was the last one to live here," I said yet again as we entered the room, dark because the shades were drawn to protect it from sun damage. "You can't underestimate the popularity of the Five Little Peppers." Truthfully, I'd never even heard of Margaret Sidney, the children's author who'd lived at the Wayside after Hawthorne, until I'd become an employee. "But luckily, we've just arrived in a room containing Hawthorne's *actual writing desk,*" I said.

The woman was out of breath, wiping her brow with the neck of her shirt. The children were slumped, the little boy scuffing his feet along the floor. I faltered. What would James do now?

I drew them to the velvet rope before the desk, stretching out my arm to the piece of wood jutting off a wall opposite a window.

"Imagine him standing there!" I exclaimed. "Alone! His back to the world! To society! To everyone and everything he knew! Imagine him trying to come up with another great sentence for another astounding story."

Nobody was buying it. It was both too much and not enough. The woman's eyes widened. "Well," she said.

"That's not a desk!" shouted the boy.

"I can't even see it," said the girl, who had barely looked up during the entire tour and who even now was looking at the floor.

"This is a scam," said the boy. "It's just a piece of *wood.*"

"Where's his chair?" said the mother.

"He wrote standing up," I said. "With his back to the window."

The mother seemed tired at the thought, and I was tired of her.

187

She should have been more impressed with Hawthorne's work ethic. Louisa May Alcott too sacrificed physical comfort for her work, switching to her left hand when her right one was tired. Most people never loved their jobs that much. I certainly didn't.

"I want to touch it!" said the boy.

"I'm sorry," I said, "but we have to stay behind this rope."

"It's awfully dark in here, isn't it, Arthur?" said the woman to her husband. I had forgotten the husband was there—he hadn't said a word during the entire tour.

"Very, very quiet," he said.

"*Dark,* I said it was *dark,* Arthur," she snapped. This reminded me, in a way, of my own parents. I waved them back toward the stairs.

"Why *is* it so dark?" said the mother.

"Well," I said, one foot still in the Sky Parlor, the other hovering over the steps that would take us downstairs, "we have to keep the shades down, as sun exposure can ruin various items in the room, bleaching them of their...historical accuracy..."

After the family departed, James sat me down in the visitors' center. "Good, very good," he said, "*and* there are just a few things I would change." It took him nearly a half hour to go through them.

During this, Ted walked in with his laid-back sway, as if he were entering his own living room. He flashed me a knowing smile as James talked. A thread of excitement zipped through me.

"My thought is, let's say, *my goal* when giving a tour," said James, "is to offer the visitors a sense of the writers who lived here, especially Hawthorne. I want them to see his life so vividly that they feel, if just for a moment, as if they themselves could stand at that writing desk all day. That's my goal. And when you give a tour, you should have your own goal too."

Would I ever give another tour, or would I be condemned to man the visitors' center forever? Maybe James would tell Audrey how bad I was, and then Audrey wouldn't let me give tours either. Audrey was an enthusiastic guide and even seemed to enjoy reciting historical facts to strangers. She was especially animated in the Sky Parlor, where I had failed so miserably. I had the sense that she felt more love for that writing desk than for any human being.

As a child, I'd loved the little women as if they were alive. I'd read my favorite parts of the book over and over in my bed on Evergreen Drive. Maybe I'd wanted to work at the Orchard to connect with that old self and those old friends. Maybe if I were giving tours of the Orchard, they'd be as good as Audrey's.

The irony of living in a tourist town is that the residents themselves rarely visit the historical sites. That was not true of me. As a child, I visited them frequently with my dad. We'd go to Walden Pond or the Old North Bridge or one of the battlefields. We'd buy lunch and sit on the grass with sandwiches, imagining the fighting that had taken place on that very spot so long ago. Sometimes, even now, I would walk the trail at the Minute Man park or wander through the graveyard at Sleepy Hollow. I could spend days jumping through eras, never quite landing in the now until Julie shook me, saying, "College! College! We're going to college!" By the end of August, she'd be in Manhattan and I'd be in Boston, but she had plans for the both of us. We'd visit each other every

other month. We'd get fake IDs. We'd have wild adventures—
"with boys!" Julie had added once with a wink, as if I were ten.

It was the summer of the diner. Julie was my ride home from
work, and we'd meet each day on Hawthorne's front lawn and
then drive far and wide in her blue Range Rover, doubling back
on our favorite diners—the kitschier the better. We'd split a piece
of cake and Julie would drink coffee while I drank Diet Coke.

Eventually, our former classmates Marcus and Raman started
joining us at the diners. Since Julie had her eye on Marcus, Raman
and I sat together by default, folding our straw wrappers into
squished accordions and then dropping water on them so they
expanded like worms. On the other side of the table, Julie and
Marcus flirted.

One day I stepped out the door of the visitors' center to meet
Julie after work and found her talking with Ted on Hawthorne's
front lawn. My heart sank. *Of course,* I thought. She'd turned our
diner trips into a dating opportunity, we were about to meet
Marcus and Raman once again, and here she was flirting with
Ted. Worse, he appeared to be flirting back. I could hear him
talking about the beautiful sunsets at Walden Pond while Julie
nodded sweetly. Her dark, silky hair fell over her shoulder and she
brushed a piece of it behind her ear with a manicured finger.

"Sounds cool," she said. "I'd love to see it sometime."

The door to the visitors' center was still in my hand, and I
closed it with a purposeful click.

"Hey, guys," I called. "Julie, you ready for your date?"

★ ★ ★

That night, post-diner, I entered my bedroom and knew by the sight of vacuum lines that my mom had been there. Now my messes were re-piled so that for a week anything I looked for would be impossible to find. My bed had been made, and on top of it sat a collection of items that I'd rather stayed lost, things that had fallen into the chasm between my bed and the wall—books from high school I'd forgotten to return, brochures from colleges I couldn't afford, and *Antigone,* the book I was supposed to read as part of a college-wide "summer books" project. "I have to read this book, *Anti-gone,*" I'd made the mistake of saying to Audrey one day. She just shook her head, scowled, and walked away, leaving me to say it again to my mother, who corrected me with a similar shake of the head. After that, I'd put off reading the book and had almost forgotten about it. Being too stupid to pronounce *Antigone* made me feel like I was too stupid for the scholarship I'd gotten. I didn't want to look at the book, so I stuffed it back under the bed.

When Julie stopped by for lunch the following week, we didn't end up talking about much. I thought maybe the week before she and Marcus had hooked up in the car during a long absence in which Raman and I, still in our booth at the diner, had rearranged our French fries into the shapes of animals, but I didn't feel like asking her about it. For one, Ted was present, which made us both self-conscious about saying anything at all. I kept stealing glances at him—undetected, I hoped. He'd come in with a stubble beard that was very attractive.

After Julie left, Ted walked over to the register, where I was stationed. I felt the top of my head as quickly and surreptitiously as I could, flattening out my frizz. He tapped his fingers on the counter, as if waiting for something.

"Yes?" I asked, trying to keep it cool.

"I don't get it," he said.

"What?"

"The Alcotts lived *here*? But I thought they lived at the Orchard?" He acted for a moment as if he were really confused, and then broke into a grin. It was a question I answered daily, since the family had lived in both homes. "You did a tour today?" he asked. "How'd it go?"

I shrugged. "Badly?" I said.

"James give you more notes? He's something else," Ted said, shaking his head. "I'm sure you were beautiful."

I resisted the urge to smile.

"You, uh, got another double date with Julie tonight?"

"It's more of a third-wheel situation," I said.

He brushed a finger against the tips of mine. My pulse quickened. "You painted your nails," he said.

"Bile green," I said, surprised he had noticed. "To match the carpeting."

This got a big laugh, which thrilled me.

"I'm thinking of going over to Walden tonight," he said. "For the sunset."

My heart practically stopped. I half expected to see Julie pop out from around the corner, snickering. But Ted and I were alone. I looked down at the register, not sure what I was supposed to say. "Cool," I chose finally.

"Yeah? Well, you should come."

"Oh, I don't know if I can," I said. I mean, *could* I just go hang out with Ted?

"You don't know if you can watch the sunset?" His lips spread into a charming smile. "Well, it's true, you aren't supposed to stare *directly* at it." He started writing his number on a stray receipt. "Seven thirty?" he said.

"Marcus texted this afternoon," Julie told me after work. "We're hitting the diner."

We were standing outside the Wayside. I looked out across the road toward the parking lot instead of at her.

"I can't," I said. "I have plans."

"*You have plans?*" Julie said. "I've known you for, what, a billion years? Have you ever made *plans*?"

"Maybe I have my own secret life you don't know about," I said.

The truth was, in our whole history together, she'd asked other people to hang out while I stood behind her like a scared younger sister, waiting for results. Besides, she was my ride. She knew everywhere I went.

"Let's just go," said Julie.

"Fine," I relented, "but I have to be back here by seven thirty." I'd asked Ted to pick me up at the Wayside. I didn't want to deal with questions from my mom.

"What for?"

I paused. "I'm meeting Ted," I said.

"*Ted?*" she said. "*You?*"

"Shush," I said, looking around. "Don't be so surprised."

"You won't even make out with Raman!" she said, as if I should just automatically want to date the best friend of whoever she was interested in. "What the hell are you gonna do with Ted?"

"Just watch the sunset," I said.

"Oh, I guess that's his big line, then," said Julie. She turned and marched off toward the parking lot, then called "Let's go" from across the road.

I walked slowly toward her with my arms crossed, like I was walking toward my mother.

We met Marcus and Raman at the diner with the mint green plastic seats and the laminate countertops covered in pink and turquoise triangles. "Hey, babe," Julie said to Marcus when we arrived, giving him a hug with one arm, her silver bracelets hanging coolly from her tiny wrist. "Been waiting long?"

I slid into the booth next to Raman. Julie talked about the Orchard as if nothing had happened between us. I kept feeling my pocket for the receipt with Ted's phone number on it, proof that he'd actually asked me out—though was it even a date? Maybe he just wanted to give me a lakeside pep talk. Maybe it was a mean trick.

I stacked the jelly packets into towers, each tower a different flavor, and then built sugar-packet roads between them.

"How adult of you," said Julie, but Raman turned around and reached across the table behind us to gather apricot jellies, handing them to me with his long fingers.

In the car, Julie and I were silent until I realized we were heading toward my house, not the Wayside. "Where are you going?" I asked.

"He's older than, like, Mr. Moreno," Julie said. Mr. Moreno

was our senior history teacher, married with two kids. "You don't even know what you're getting into."

"You've got to be kidding me," I said. I felt dizzy with anger.

"Look, you can do whatever you want," she said, "but I won't be any part of it." As if she had spent a lifetime taking the high road.

"You're just jealous," I said. "You thought he was going to ask you out."

"Dude," Julie said, "just because I was flirting with him doesn't mean I want to date him. Unlike you, I flirt sometimes."

I sat in the passenger seat seething. I felt like I was fourteen again, arguing with my mom in the car.

I didn't even have my own cell phone to call him and cancel. Of course Julie had one. She had everything first: a computer, the internet, her period, a car, a boyfriend.

"Give me your cell so I can tell him I can't go, at least," I said. She reached into her purse without taking her eyes off the road and practically threw her phone at me. I felt dumb and defeated calling him in front of Julie, asking for a rain check.

The visitors' center was still locked. I leaned against the building, eating my bagel, and then decided to look for James. When I turned the corner at the back of the Wayside, I saw him atop a metal ladder stretched to the roof of the house, talking to a man who stood at its base.

"No one seems to care about the maintenance of this house," James told the man. His voice was as close to annoyed as I'd ever heard it.

"We do, we do care about the maintenance of our historical

houses very much. It's just that we have not hired or paid you specifically to clean the gutters, so I ask you to please get down from there."

"If I don't clean these gutters, who will?" asked James. He leaned precariously far from the ladder to pull off a piece of peeling paint with his fingers. "The government paint job has not fared too well, *and* it was done only three years ago!" He dropped the paint chip and watched it flutter down to the man's feet.

"Sir, it's a liability issue. I'm really gonna need you to get down."

I waited for James to do his thing: big smile, popped eyes, impassioned lecture against those who let historic sites die: "This is the only National Historic Site to have housed *three* literary heroes!," et cetera.

But what he did was look at the sky. "I'm not sure how you're going to get me down from here," James said, "if I decide not to come down."

"Seriously?" said the man.

James and the man were silent.

"Look, sir," the man said finally. "I don't want to do this, but I can have you fired. Is that what you want? Will that get the house painted? Will that clean the gutters?"

"So fire me," said James.

"Just come down," said the man.

James looked down at the man. He looked at the sky. He looked down again.

Finally, he took a deep breath and began stepping down the ladder.

When he got to the bottom, he shook the man's hand. "I'm

sure you can see that maintenance is a big issue here, and I know you're just doing what you've got to do."

"Sorry, sir," the man kept saying as he helped James put away the ladder.

I ducked back around the corner of the house, embarrassed for James, who was so concerned about the dreary house of dead authors that most people have never read or even thought about.

I waited for James at the door of the visitors' center, pretending I hadn't seen a thing. When he came to unlock it, his smile was as broad as it had always been, and he was whistling.

It threw me off guard. But I said, "Are you always this happy?," something I'd become accustomed to saying almost every morning.

"No," he said with a smile as he let us in.

"I'm going out after dinner," I told my dad as we ate leftover spaghetti from white Styrofoam boxes. "With friends."

"Can't you go on your mother's nights? She only has six of them," he said.

"It's a Friday," I said.

"Did you get your room assignment for fall yet?"

Jesus, I thought. Despite not speaking to each other, it sometimes seemed like my parents coordinated their questions so I had to say everything twice. "Not yet," I said.

"You should call them, make sure they have your registration stuff."

"Mm-hmm," I said. I bit a meatball in half, the middle still cold.

"Are the dorms coed?"

"I think so," I said.

"The bathrooms too?"

"I don't know."

"Let's hope they aren't—guys are disgusting."

I nodded.

"Let me know when you find out. I can call the school if it doesn't come soon."

"I'm sure it'll come soon," I said, though I'd only just mailed the forms.

My dad ate a piece of day-old garlic bread in nearly one bite. "So, has he tried something on you yet?"

"What?"

"You know, the man at work who is *very nice*."

"Oh come on," I said. For a second I'd thought he'd meant Ted. "He wouldn't do anything. He really is just very nice."

"You don't know the power of a young woman on a man." He paused, thinking. "Parmesan cheese!" he said. "I knew we forgot something."

I couldn't get the image of James up on that ladder out of my head. James cared for the Wayside the way my father had once cared for the battlefields. We used to lie on our backs in the deep grassy field near the Old North Bridge, which arched its way elegantly over the calm Concord River, and we'd watch the white clouds float through the sky. Though this was where soldiers had bled and died, the place was peaceful, like the quiet eye of a storm. The first shot of the Revolutionary War had been fired here, one bullet I imagined flying slo-mo through the air, setting in motion events that had led America to now. Europe and Asia had sites that were thousands of years old, but this is what we had, this was our history. Funny that Frank almost never came with us, and now there he was, halfway across the globe on a sandy battlefield of his own. Had he really gone that far to get away from us?

I thought about the place we used to live, my childhood home, a little rectangle set on a gentle green slope, with burnt-red siding and a gray shingled roof. It had long ago been bought, invaded, remodeled. I missed it. The Old North Bridge, those battlefields—they were as close as I could get now to going home.

Ted picked me up at around seven.

I'd changed into a blue dress.

"This a date?" my father asked like it was a joke, but I could tell that he thought I looked nice. He waved at Ted from the window. "Is he going to come up?"

"No," I said, giving my father a kiss on the cheek.

"Sorry about that," I said in the car.

"About what?"

"The waving," I said.

"Not a problem," said Ted.

We arrived at Walden just before sunset. A breeze carried the scent of pine needles and pond. People were speckled across the beach, leaning back on blankets and chairs, layering on T-shirts and shorts over swimsuits as it cooled. I wondered what Ted and I looked like walking together. Did people wonder what I was doing here with this handsome, older guy? Or did they wonder what he was doing here with me?

Ted was telling me about his research, how in the early 1700s a minuteman had lived on the Wayside property, how in the late 1700s enemy troops had marched right past on their way to the Old North Bridge. I kept saying "Cool" and "Wow" as if I had no other vocabulary.

We walked past Thoreau's cabin, which might have been the only place in the Greater Boston area smaller than my father's apartment. It had a sign out front: I WENT TO THE WOODS BECAUSE I WISHED TO LIVE DELIBERATELY, TO FRONT ONLY THE ESSENTIAL FACTS OF LIFE.

The essential facts of life? What were they? Thoreau had never been a seventeen-year-old girl.

We sat down on the sand. I zigzagged my finger up and down the space next to me, hardly leaving a trail because the sand caved in on itself. A hazy reflection of pine trees and low, pink clouds floated in the water. The sun bubbled over the tree line.

"Hey," Ted said, taking my hand. When I looked at him, he looked at me right back. Right in the eyes. "This is nice, right?" I wanted to look away, look out into the water or at the children building fortresses in the sand. "You know why I invited you here?" he asked. I shook my head no. "It's because you're funny," he said. "Plus, you're pretty cute."

"Come on," I said, still zigzagging my finger through the sand. "We all know Julie's the cute one."

"I mean, sure, she's attractive," Ted said seriously. "But I don't know. You aren't trying so fucking hard." Ironic, because I felt like I *was* trying pretty hard. "Julie thinks she's special," said Ted, "but you're oblivious to how special you are."

I couldn't help but smile.

After sunset, we sat in his car. I was so nervous that I could feel my hands shaking. When we kissed, I felt light-headed and robotic. Where was my tongue supposed to go? What was I supposed to do with his tongue, which was in my mouth? What about this buildup of spit? Was I messing everything up? I was, wasn't I?

When our faces parted I was blushing, but Ted pretended not to notice.

When he put his hand on my thigh, near the edge of my dress, I went stiff.

"Hold on," I said.

"What?" he said. He didn't take his hand away.

"I don't know."

"What don't you know?" he asked.

The truth was, I hadn't bargained for more than a kiss, and I didn't know how to proceed. Maybe Julie had predicted this. *Of course* he wanted more than a kiss. He'd probably been with dozens of women. He'd lived *two* of my lives. He was old enough to be married, divorced, and married again.

I wondered what my parents would think if they knew I was here. Maybe nothing. This is exactly what my father expected from a guy. What about James? What would he think?

"Julie just—I don't know," I said. "She thought it was a bad idea. Like, because...I don't know. Well, you're older than me, I think."

"You came here for a reason," he said. "I guarantee Julie is fucking with you because of her own shit. You're an adult, May. You can make your own decisions."

Maybe he really didn't know how old I was. Regardless, I didn't feel like an adult. When someone referred to me as a woman, I looked around to see who they were talking about.

"You just need to relax," said Ted. "Don't let Julie make your decisions for you."

I did need to relax. I needed to reset, try again when I wasn't so nervous. "We should probably leave anyway," I said, looking out the window at the emptying parking lot.

"That's what you want?" he asked. "Your decision," he said. He waited until I nodded to take his hand off my leg.

When I got home that night, my mother was sitting at the table, which was set for dinner with utensils and two blue cloth placemats. "Hey," I said. Only when she didn't respond did I notice that her cheeks were glistening under our fluorescent kitchen light. She was staring out the window, oblivious to my presence. I didn't want to move or speak again, for fear of alarming her.

But finally, quietly, I asked, "Are you okay?"

"Your brother"—how quickly a heart stops—"is getting married."

My whole body seemed to go soft. I wanted to melt into the kitchen floor or get down on my knees and thank the Lord I didn't really believe in or smack my mother's wet cheek. My mother sobbed, a hand covering the side of her face nearer me, as if that would prevent me from seeing or hearing her.

"What's the matter?" I said. "Who's he marrying?"

She kept crying and then stopped with the noise of a stalled car, grabbing a napkin and wiping her face, still not looking at me. "A woman in the army," she said. "He's really gone, May," she said. "He's not coming back."

"What do you mean?" I said. "His tour's almost over!" But the relief I'd felt a moment earlier had already disappeared.

One afternoon at the visitors' center, Audrey took the jar of pickles from her brown paper bag to make sure the lid was screwed on. One of the visitors laughed. "I used to bring jars of pickles like that to work when I was pregnant with my first," she said. "People thought I was crazy."

Audrey's eyes flashed. "I am not pregnant!" she shouted. "Simply because I am overweight and twenty-seven does not mean I am having a child or am married or have a boyfriend. I'm single, and I want to be single! Can't anyone just accept that I like pickles?"

I had never seen Audrey like this before. The handful of other visitors in the room looked down at their feet. The lady who had spoken took a cautious step backward. "That's fine," she said. "That's fine."

Audrey looked around at everyone not looking at her. "What?" she cried, and then she walked right out the door.

"Um," I announced. "The next tour will begin in approximately thirty-five minutes. Audrey, the tour guide, is having a rough day, but she'll be better after lunch, I'm sure." Then I left to find Audrey, who was sitting on the front lawn, eating her pickles fiercely, juice flying everywhere.

"Audrey!" I yelled.

"What?" said Audrey, taking another savage bite. "You're supposed to be in the visitors' center! Did you put up the sign? It's my lunch break now!" She looked like she was going to continue speaking, but instead she stopped, ate the remaining half of a pickle in one bite, and wiped her mouth with her arm.

"You're scaring away the visitors, Audrey! Nobody said you were pregnant. God!"

"Fuck you," said Audrey.

She wiped the wet edges of each eye with her wrist, which only made them appear wetter because her temples were now slicked with pickle juice. "My twelfth rejection," she said. "Count them! Count to twelve! You can't! You don't have enough fingers!"

"What are you talking about?" I said.

She didn't look at me, seemed to be speaking to the air. "I'll never be a broadcast journalist. I'm too fat." It occurred to me that even if Audrey had been overweight when I met her— and that was debatable—she certainly wasn't anymore. She was getting thin and, perhaps, even *green*.

"I thought you were going to be a writer-journalist," I said.

She snorted. "I am," she said. "I'm going to write my stories, and then broadcast them. But not if I don't get a job! Not if I've been rejected by twelve stations! And I'm not pregnant! There is absolutely no possible way I will ever be pregnant!"

"You can't get pregnant?" I asked.

"Forget it," she said. "I'm going to end up just like Christine, I know it. If I ever get a job, it will all end up that way."

I didn't know who Christine was, but I knew Audrey had a habit of referring to famous people as near acquaintances, like her good friends Louisa and Nathaniel. "Christine?" I asked, taking the bait.

"Christine Chubbuck! A woman you would know if you had any interest at all in broadcast journalism!"

I had almost no interest at all in broadcast journalism.

"She committed suicide on live television during her broadcast. She was twenty-nine and lonely and depressed and she never dated and she told everyone she was going to kill herself, and then she did, on live television. At least she became famous!" Audrey stuffed an entire, final pickle in her mouth, and it snapped in two on its way in. Then she crumbled the brown paper bag into a ball and just sat there. I returned to an empty visitors' center.

I followed Audrey on her next tour, to make sure she was okay. In the Sky Parlor, one of the tourists asked why the shades were drawn. Audrey explained it beautifully, fully composed and without a trace of her earlier outburst. A woman wanted to touch Hawthorne's desk, and even though the meaning of a velvet rope should have been obvious, Audrey calmly explained why no one could touch the desk. "Not even the staff who work here have touched it," she said. I wondered if that was true, if Audrey or James had never touched the desk they so admired, if they had ever hoped that luck, directly from the site of creation, could rub off on them.

Ted picked me up a block from my mom's house, at a place he probably assumed was my actual address. I'd never done this sort of thing in high school, and I felt like I was getting something essential out of the way.

We went to a diner Julie and I had long ago deemed far too un-kitsch, with its dearth of aluminum and its boring white linoleum tabletops. I'd already eaten, so I just ordered a Diet Coke and fries. Ted ordered a massive two-patty hamburger with sweet potato fries, coleslaw, and a side salad.

"You think you have enough food there?" I asked, trying to be funny and flirty and casual, or whatever I was supposed to be.

He nodded. "Gotta watch out, though," he said, tapping his stomach. "Not so young anymore."

I split my fries into pieces so I would eat them slowly, sucking the salt and grease from each piece before eating the next. Ted was talking about his graduate program, how museum studies was housed in three different departments, how his department was really the most important.

I spent most of the meal feeling grateful that he was still hanging out with me. I asked him questions about the program, hoping to avoid talking about myself. I was afraid that anything I might say—about living with my mom, about dinners with my dad, about going away to college—would either reveal to him or remind him of my youth. I managed to remind him anyway as I stacked the butter pats into a four-walled tower. "Cute," he said.

We made out in the car, but it still didn't feel natural. I kept changing the position of my hands, first putting them on his shoulders like I was slow dancing, then moving them to his back.

"You're very pretty," he whispered in my ear. "You just gotta let go a little bit."

This was probably true. I probably did have to let go. I let his hands creep up my thigh, up my shirt, to the back of my bra, which I felt click open.

"Wait," I said.

"For what?" he whispered.

"Not now," I said. Was this really how fast adults went?

"When, though?" he said.

"Really," I said, moving away from him, trying and failing to clip my bra back together with one hand.

Ted put his hands on the steering wheel and stared out the front window. "You know," he said, "I want to be honest with you. I kinda feel like I'm being jerked around. Like you want the attention, but then you back away. Which, where does that leave me? What do I get from that?"

Why was I always in the passenger seat of a car, feeling like a kid in trouble? One of us had misjudged my potential. I felt like I was being dropped off at the bottom of the Alps when I was still learning to ride a bike. What I wanted was to go slower, but you didn't ask a thirty-whatever if he would go slower. You just had to catch up, pretend you were right there the whole time.

He started the car. "I like you, obviously," he said. "I wouldn't be hanging out with you if I didn't. But you have to make a decision about what you want." He lowered the hand brake and started backing out of the parking space. "Because other people get tired," he said. "Their interest wanes."

What was I supposed to do? I thought of the lifetime I'd spent listening to advice from my parents and teachers and friends, from song lyrics and TV shows and movies: Go for it. Just say no. Seize the day. Trust your instincts. What was my instinct? I felt like a deer in headlights, trapped in the middle of the road, unwilling to go forward or back.

Was there really middle ground here? We weren't going to go

"part way." It was not, as they say, horseshoes and hand grenades. It was more like: you either passed a test or you failed it, you won a game or you lost it, you were a virgin or you weren't.

All of a sudden it hit me, what Audrey had really meant by saying she couldn't be pregnant.

James decided to take me on a "one-on-one practice tour." He said I'd "gotten the facts and stories" and he wanted to work on "the nuances." On our way around the house, he talked about his life, still smiling: a wife who had long ago died of cancer, a grown son who visited often, his writing career which hadn't, just yet, taken off. "Can you *really* be this happy?" I asked him again.

"Why can't you believe that? Tell me: you're so young and why can't you believe that?" Something was bothering me. Something about how he was always smiling, about how he seemed to believe that "and"—that words at all—could ward off negativity like a cast spell. I told James I'd seen him on the ladder, that I knew he couldn't've been happy then. "But when you came down to unlock the visitors' center, you didn't know I'd seen and you were whistling again, just like that! Wasn't that fake?"

"I don't want to bring down morale here. The gutters, the peeling paint, the shades—they bring down morale enough." He nodded to himself. "I can see how my smile might feel like a lie to you, *and*—"

"*But,*" I said.

"*And,*" he said with a laugh, "I don't mean it like that. For me it's...aspirational."

"Sounds like a lot of work."

"I'm glad we've had this summer to get to know each other," he said. "I think it's important to find friendships with people of all ages and types, so you can understand the world in contexts other than your own. That's why reading is so important. That's why writing is so important."

When we arrived in the Sky Parlor, James shook his head. "I just wish we could pull the shades up! How wonderful it would be, to look at the things as Hawthorne did!"

It did seem ridiculous, this order to keep the shades down, an order given by the same people who refused to repaint the house. No wonder the place was so dreary. No wonder visitors were unimpressed: we were blocking out the light and the view! It wasn't fair to the house, or to history, or to James, or to me. The darkness made the house seem unreal, a caricature of what it once was. Why had the Orchard been given more grant money than the Wayside? The Orchard's shades stayed up and sunlight poured through special protective windows. It was as if the Wayside had literally been put by the wayside because it wasn't special or interesting enough, the loser of some literary popularity contest that I had cast a vote in by wishing I was working at the Orchard.

I realized I admired James. He managed himself the way he tried to manage the Wayside: clean the gutters, paint the siding, and step by step it might all one day be as good as he dreamed.

"Do you ever lift the shades?" I asked. "Have you ever? I would love to see them lifted."

He paused for a moment. "I have," he said. I looked around the room, imagining it swallowed by light. "Just briefly, just quickly.

I wouldn't want to ruin anything. I think it's important for the house to feel, sometimes, the way it once was."

I walked over to the velvet rope, swinging it back and forth. "What about his desk?" I asked.

"Don't tell," James said. "But I stood there. I touched it. I felt like a writer. People can be connected like that, through things and places. I wish everyone could see this room that way, could have that feeling." But he did not invite me to see it that way, perhaps because I had no aspirations of becoming a writer.

Now when I saw Ted he nodded his head at me like teachers used to do when they passed you in the hallway and couldn't remember your name. I flashed him a quick, awkward smile and looked back down at the register, my face burning.

Later, James asked, "How are you getting along with the folks here at work?"

"What do you mean?"

"Julie hasn't been coming around. You don't seem to talk to Ted anymore."

I shrugged, but I was surprised he'd noticed. I'd barely talked to Ted at work in the first place.

"Ted's a lot older than you," James said.

"We were hardly ever even friends," I said.

"And Julie?"

"I don't know," I said, which was the truth. The rest of the truth was that work was starting to feel lonely. I gave tours and tried to think of my goals, but I didn't have any. I punched the keys on the register one at a time like a typist who doesn't know where any of the keys are, and I abandoned my barrettes and headbands, letting my hair do whatever it wanted. I surrendered, finally, to *Antigone,* wanting to give it a chance like I'd never really given Hawthorne. If Audrey was Hester Prynne, maybe I was Antigone, my brother away at a war nobody in Boston believed in, and he was fighting it for me and he was fighting it for them and he was fighting it most of all for himself, and it didn't matter what I believed in besides my brother, besides believing that he believed in what he was fighting for, and I thought, sure, I would sacrifice myself for him if it came to that.

Some days were so hot and humid that being outside seemed to switch off my brain. The drives to work with Julie were quiet and sad. She stopped asking me to go out with Marcus and Raman. "That Ted thing is over anyway," I said to her one day, and just getting it out of my throat felt like a defeat. After that, she started smiling at Ted again, flipping her hair back and forth in his presence, but she hardly said a word to me.

Audrey was sitting on Hawthorne's front lawn when I arrived at work one Friday morning. This was unusual. She was wearing a low-cut white shirt, a little loose on her now, with a red, scripted *A* in the corner. She kept taking something out of her pocket and rubbing her fingers below her eyes. It took me several glances to realize that she was just putting on makeup.

When Audrey came into the visitors' center I could see that she was wearing both mascara and eyeliner, thick and dark as if she were going to a nightclub. She had half-moons of makeup under both of her eyes, her foundation a shade too light. She took out her compact again and rubbed a finger under the bottom rim of both eyes until I blurted out "It's fine!" for fear of it getting cakier.

"You take the tours today," she said, smacking her makeup container shut.

During my tours I tried to work the magic that James had taught me, but my jokes fell flat. In a morning group of elderly women, only two advanced to the Sky Parlor, and by the time they got there, they were too tired to be interested. Around lunchtime a young girl on a small tour said loudly to her mother, "The other house was better."

In the late afternoon, a new tour gathered: a family of four, a senior couple, and a youngish professorial guy. Audrey hadn't spoken to me since that morning, had simply sat in the register chair as if it were her throne, reading a novel and surveying the tourists. But now she jumped up. "I'm doing a tour," she said.

I followed behind the group. She toured with her usual ease, but I was uneasy. I led the guests down from the Sky Parlor and back to the visitors' center. When I got downstairs, I realized Audrey was missing.

"Is someone still up there?" I asked, though it wasn't that unusual for an interested party to hang back with the guide, ask a few more questions after the tour was over.

I rang up a few books, then sat back at the register, wondering what was going on with Audrey. Just as I got up to see if she was returning, I saw a man, the professorial guy, exiting the house, power walking toward the parking lot. I was running out to the front lawn to find out what was going on when I heard Audrey. "It's free!" she was yelling. "It's free! I promise, I won't tell anyone!"

I watched her run out the front door, her breasts and small gut bobbing up and down. It didn't really hit me that she was naked until she stopped, suddenly, in the middle of the lawn. The guy was gone but she whispered anyway, "You can have me. Don't you want me? Don't you want me? Who wants me?" She sat down right there on the lawn, her head curled up to her knees, her entire body rocking back and forth, a giant sob bursting from her as sudden as a firework.

"Audrey!" I yelled. I looked for something to cover her with, but there was nothing nearby. Where were her clothes? "Audrey," I said. "What happened? Let's get your clothes." I put my arm in the nook of her elbow and made a motion like we should stand up, but she wouldn't move. She didn't push me away, she didn't yell, she just kept sobbing, louder and louder.

People had gathered, watching or staring or pointing or walking swiftly back to the parking lot. I let go of Audrey and stood right in front of her. "Hey, you," I yelled to a woman who was staring, wide-eyed. "Go in the house and find her clothes." The woman just stood there, looking around her. "Yeah, you!" I shouted. "Come on!"

The woman returned with Audrey's clothes, which, she said, had been inside one of the bedrooms, but they turned out to be useless because Audrey wouldn't budge. Finally, I asked a bystander for a phone and called 911. I couldn't think of anything else to do.

"Wow!" said my dad as soon as he opened the door. "You're a star! That story is everywhere!"

The local news station had arrived on the scene soon after the ambulance, and I'd mumbled a few meaningless words in front of the camera.

"Slow news day," I said. Really, though—slow news day? We were fighting two wars. And what could the news ever know about Audrey? Audrey, who, I supposed, for years and years had carried around what she hadn't done like a weight that had finally crushed her.

"She just ran straight out of the house, no clothes?"

"I guess," I said.

"Where is she now? Mental institution?"

"I guess," I said.

"What? You didn't like her. That's what you said, wasn't it? That she was mean."

"That's not the point," I said.

The phone rang and my dad answered it. "Hello?" he said. "Yeah, she's here." But he didn't hand me the phone. "Sounds like the lady went off the deep end," he said into the phone. "You must have a lot of red tape over there with the whole incident." My dad nodded. "Yeah, okay, here she is."

"How are you?" asked James. He must have found the number in my emergency contacts.

"I'm okay," I said.

"You did a good thing there."

"I don't feel like I did much of anything."

"You did. You were there for her," said James. "I wanted to let you know that I talked to Audrey's parents. She's going to spend the night at the hospital, then go home. She won't be coming back, though. To the Wayside, I mean. If you're willing, you and I can tag team and fill in for Audrey, keep the ship up and running."

I was happy he'd asked me, even though there was no one else to ask.

"I'm glad you were there today," he said. "Call me if you need anything, okay? I'll let you get back to it."

As soon as I hung up the phone, my dad said, "He does seem very nice."

"He really is."

For a moment neither of us spoke. "Are you sure he doesn't want to get in—I mean, you're a woman now. Are you sure he isn't after you or something?"

"Dad, shut up."

The room fell silent. I looked down at my hands, the white crescents of my fingernails chewed nearly to nothing. I thought of Julie's nails, how she let them grow, glossed them clear so that even in the diner's dimness they each reflected a thin, white strip of light that floated back and forth across her nails as she moved her hands. How could you tell a girl from a woman? It wasn't age, anyway.

I couldn't do this tonight—this small room, this small meal, these small boxes. Was there anyone left in this town besides James who I even remotely understood?

"I forgot," I said. "I have plans. I need to use the phone. It's late."

In some other time, I would've called Julie. And in some other time before that, I would've knocked on Frank's door, let him push me around a little.

I called Ted.

215

"May?" he asked, like he'd forgotten who I was.

"May," I said again. "I'm ready. To go out. Walden."

"Now?"

"Yeah."

"The sun's already setting," he said.

"Just pick me up."

Before I left, my dad looked out the window from the sink where he was rinsing off a pile of plastic utensils. Ted had grown a new goatee that made him look older. "Which friend is that?" he asked, his thumb rubbing the dent of a spoon. "I don't remember him."

As soon as I got in the car I told Ted, "We can sneak in, on the far side of the lake." I'd never done it myself, but it was a well-known entry point among high schoolers when Walden closed after dark.

"What do you suggest I do with the car?" Ted asked.

"You don't have to go," I said. "You can drop me off at my mom's." But I didn't feel like going back to my mom's. I put my hand on his thigh. I didn't look at him. It's funny, how quickly you learn what bargaining chips you have.

"My mom's house is nearby," said Ted. "We can get bikes from there." I hadn't known his mom still lived around there.

His mom's house was a giant white rectangle with a red front door. Ted tapped a number into the keypad and the garage door hummed open. He rolled a bike toward me, one where the center bar faded from dark pink to purple. "My little sister's," he said.

"You have a sister?"

"Stepsister, actually," he said. "At boarding school. Well, camp for the summer, or, really, some kind of course in New York. I forget the specifics." He rolled out his own bike from behind a garbage can of sports balls.

"How old is she?"

"Fifteen? No, sixteen. Like your age."

My stomach dropped. He thought I was even *younger* than I actually was?

Ted sped out in front of me, looking back to make sure I was keeping up. I rode in his wake, happy to be outside, helmetless, moving. My sweat cooled as the darkness came in. We left our bikes by the road and snuck quietly through the woods.

By the time we were on the shore the sun had long disappeared below the horizon. Only the thinnest sliver of moon and the dots of stars lit our way. We stood close to each other, our hands clasped, walking slowly and silently across the sand. When we reached the water Ted bent down and felt it with his hand, then took off his shoes and put in his feet. I put my feet in too. The water was warm from the hot day, warmer than the air.

"Let's go in," he said. Before I could answer, he had let go of my hand and begun taking off his clothes. I squinted in the dark. He was not one of the hairless creatures I'd been friends with in high school, though I had never seen them naked.

He had a trace of a six-pack. A thin trail of dark hair led down from his navel. I felt like I wasn't so much here on this beach but watching a movie. It was Julie who should have been with a man who looked like this, who should have been with a man at all. Or Audrey—maybe she should have had this.

"Come on," said Ted.

"I am," I said, though I hadn't moved. *Sixteen?* I kept thinking. What did it matter? It was practically true. Why did I care if he was taking advantage of my age? Maybe I was double-crossing him, getting something I wanted too.

I waited until he got in, and then I took off my clothes with as little ceremony as possible and got into the water, where the reflected moon reminded me of Julie's fingernails.

Ted swam perfect freestyle back and forth, and I doggie-paddled in place until he came up behind me, feeling my wet back with his hands, and bringing them further, cupping my breasts. He whispered in my ear, "The shore?"

I nodded in the dark. Maybe pretending that you knew what you were doing and actually knowing what you were doing were almost the same thing.

I lay on my back, the sand sticking to everything wet, which was all of me. He fished around in his pile of clothes to get to his pants pocket.

"Relax," he said as I closed my eyes, "this is the fun part," and he didn't say much else after that.

How quickly the things you hear so much about are over, and how little you need to be a part of them.

We lay there for a minute. The sand itched, had invaded every crevice of my body. I shivered. Ted's breathing was heavy, but mine was shallow. I tried to listen to my own breath, just so that my heart would beat slower.

He rolled away from me. "Let's rinse off," he said.

He jumped right in, but I got up slowly. All of the blood in my head rushed down to my feet. I felt dizzy. I squinted toward the ground below me. Even in the night I could see the dark spot in the sand.

Did all rites of passage include blood? Men and women went to war and spilled blood, and teenage girls spilled their own blood just like this. It seemed stupid. Still, I wished for a moment that I could keep it, some proof in case I didn't believe myself in the morning.

Earlier that year, during all of those rallies protesting the newest war, I had seen a college student with punky pink hair and a nose ring carrying a sign written in different-colored Sharpies, peace signs in the Os: FIGHTING FOR PEACE IS LIKE FUCKING FOR VIRGINITY, it said. Behind her stood a slew of others, holding signs made from ripped cardboard boxes, saying MAKE LOVE NOT WAR. They chanted it, over and over, as if the two were opposites, as if one prevented the other. But sometimes making love was like heading into battle, and maybe for my brother heading into battle was like making love.

"Come on," Ted called into the darkness.

I rubbed the spot away with my foot and dashed into the water. Despite how warm it was, my teeth clicked together in a shiver that I couldn't seem to stop.

I awoke the next morning scratching sand out of my ear, and I thought of my brother, who, on his first tour of Afghanistan, had written home, "It's hot and sandy as hell. I don't own anything without sand in it." I wished he were here right now, not just so I could be sure he was safe or so I could meet his fiancée, but so he could attend a Styrofoam Dinner, could look out the window from my father's place and say, "Hey, how old is that guy?," because he would know the right questions to ask.

Once, when Frank was in high school, he pinned me against the wall of our house. I had been hanging out with a girl two years my senior who had been caught smoking cigarettes behind his school, among other things.

"You stop hanging out with that girl," he'd said to me.

"Why?" I said, struggling to get out of his grip. He already had muscles like the Hulk.

"She does all kinds of stupid shit," he said.

"Let go of me!" I said, making a new attempt to get free. "I'll yell," I said.

He put a preemptive hand over my mouth, I spit into it, and he promptly wiped my own spit across my face. "Listen, you stop hanging out with her or I'll tell Mom and Dad."

"They won't care."

"If they don't care, I'll find some other way to make your life miserable."

"It's not fair," I said. "You can't control me."

"Listen," he said, letting me go. "The truth is, you're cooler than she is. So just shut up, get over it, and do this one thing for me." The funny part is, I was relieved. I had an excuse. Maybe part of me wanted to be the kind of person who smoked cigarettes behind the high school, but it turned out that I didn't actually want to smoke cigarettes behind the high school.

★ ★ ★

I thought Ted might call on Saturday, but he didn't. On Sunday morning, I called Julie and asked if we could all go out for brunch, the four of us, like we used to. I didn't even feel like I was giving in. I was just tired of being alone. We went to the diner that Julie and I didn't like, the one Ted had taken me to. "Marcus likes to go here," said Julie. "He says it's fancier." She'd forgotten the whole point of going to the diners in the first place.

"So," Julie had said in the car. "Audrey must have been insane all along. I knew she was kind of crazy, but this just proved it. It's too perfect."

"You could probably stop making fun of her, Julie."

"Jesus Christ, May. You've had a stick up your ass all summer. What happened to you?"

Our table was spectacularly white, like milk. I kept putting my finger in my ear and finding sand. A few grains spilled onto the white table, standing out like little periods on a blank sheet of paper.

"Are you all right?" Raman asked after I'd torn apart several packets of sugar, first dumping the sugar into the coffee I'd ordered, and then shredding the paper.

"Fine," I said. "Tired."

The coffee was terrible, but I downed the whole thing anyway. "See?" said Julie. "It's not so bad."

It was so bad. What was bad was that life was all about waiting for adult things to get less bad. Children were smart: they just liked things that were already good, like swing sets and cereals with marshmallows and candy shaped like bears.

A group walked in, sat a few booths behind us, and started laughing and talking. They looked eons older than us.

I kept looking back at them. I could picture Ted among them, maybe with his arm around the pretty one with the shiny brown hair.

"Really, are you all right?" Raman asked again.

Julie was stirring her coffee with a little red straw. She'd drunk only half of it, not even. Raman was onto his second Sprite. "Maybe it's the coffee," said Julie. "May's not used to drinking coffee."

"I'm used to more than you think I'm used to," I snarled, in far too Audreyish a fashion.

I went home and I went to bed. I stayed in my room until that evening, when the phone rang. Since my mother was out for groceries, I had to go into the kitchen in my underwear to answer it. Maybe it was Ted.

"Hello?" I said.

"Heyyy," said a faraway voice that I recognized immediately.

"Frank!" I yelled. "Frank, you should come home!"

"Home, man? I'm getting hitched."

"Yeah," I said. "I've heard. So crazy. Congrats!"

"You're gonna love Shelley," he said.

"Yeah," I replied, putting on my tour voice. "I can't wait—we all can't wait." *All?* As if in his absence we had become some kind of family unit. "We want to see you and her and, you know, have you shove wedding cake in each other's mouths."

"I'm sure you'd love that," said Frank. "Is Mom there?"

"No, she's getting groceries. She's gonna be pissed she missed you."

"Shelley's calling card has been fucking up and she's been using mine to call her family, so there's, like, no minutes left. So I have to go pretty soon anyway."

"Man," I said, but I didn't know what to say next.

"Are you all ready for school?"

"Eh."

"You're gonna love it," he said. "You're gonna be fine. What are you doing all summer? Hanging with Julie?"

"Kind of," I said. "She's being annoying."

"Well, Julie was always kind of a fucktard," he said. "What's the place you're working at again?"

"The Wayside."

"That fucking place," he said.

"Yeah," I said. What could you say in a two-minute phone call?

"Look, I should go. Tell Mom I'll call her soon."

"All right," I said. "Love you."

And I knew my mom was right. He'd gone to the Middle East to get away from us, and he was finally returning now only because he'd be returning with a new wife, and with her he'd find a new family, a new home.

When I finally returned to the Wayside after the weekend, for the first time since Audrey's incident, I felt somehow like I hadn't been there for an eternity. Everything should have changed, but it hadn't. The plaster statues had not stopped smiling, they had not stopped being in the middle of the actions they had always been in the middle of and always would be in the middle of, and even the books had not stopped being stacked as neatly as Audrey had left them. The paint had not stopped peeling, the furniture had not escaped from any rooms, and the visitors had not stopped coming. In fact, there were more of them. I answered questions concerning Audrey as calmly and tactfully as I thought she would have herself.

"You're doing a great job with the tours," James said as I swept random spots on the floor whether they were dirty or not. "How are you doing?"

"Everything is just different now, even though nothing has changed," I admitted. I pushed the frizzy hair up at the nape of my neck. I swear there was still sand in my hair, or maybe I was imagining it.

"Things are different," said James. He sat down in front of the register. "Seeing someone you know get so out of touch with reality like that, that had to be a shock."

I wanted to tell him about Ted, tell him I had just done it to get it done with, to be Julie, to not be Audrey, to find out if that was the difference between the last piece of my life and the next, but that I didn't find out anything. Sometimes the only difference between doing something and not doing something was what you could claim later.

"Audrey and I didn't even get along," I said.

"It doesn't matter," he said. "It's still allowed to affect you."

"I don't even think she ever touched Hawthorne's writing desk."

"Few people have," said James. He stood up and put his hand gently, kindly, on my shoulder and then took it away.

A little later, Ted arrived. "Hey," was all he said, nodding toward me.

"Hey," I replied without smiling.

When James was off leading a tour, Ted and I spoke.

"All right," he said. "You mad or something?"

"Should I be?" I said.

"Look," he said. "To be honest, I didn't really feel like you were into it that much."

"Whatever," I said. "We're finished anyway."

"We weren't even—I mean, it works differently when you're older, you know?" He had finally played the age card.

"Okay," I said. I didn't want to be with him, yet every word out of my mouth felt like a concession.

"And *you* called me," he said.

"*Okay,*" I said.

"All right," he said.

I restocked books with a kind of vengeance. "Thank you for coming," I said tersely to our guests, throwing down their purchases. I wanted to get out of there. I wanted to get out of suburbia and Boston and Massachusetts and the summer and the heat and my teens.

But I couldn't leave any of it, no matter what I did. Even on the last tour block of the day, any hope of closing early was foiled by some tourists on their final literary stop of the afternoon, a young woman and her father. I assumed she went to Brown, since that's what her T-shirt said. James's broad smile stretched across his face. I was reminded of those first days when I thought the smile might snap off and take on a life of its own. "You two are lucky," he said, rubbing his hands together. "A private tour! As you probably know, this is the home of—"

"Oh, she knows," said the father.

"Ah," said James, who put his hands to his temples and closed his eyes for a moment as if she were a little kid. "You're a writer, aren't you?"

"Yes," she said. "Or I want to be."

"Don't let her fool you," said the father. "She's very talented."

"Thank you, Dad," she said.

For a moment I felt like this was the same girl—the eight-year-old writer—who had walked in that first week of the summer. I felt like I'd been working at the Wayside for so long that she'd already grown up.

"Do you have a favorite Hawthorne work?" asked James.

"Well, there's always 'Young Goodman Brown,'" she said.

"Excellent choice!" said James. I'd been with him enough this summer that I could read the different permutations of his happiness, and finding a fellow reader and writer was its own category of joy.

They began their private tour, and I stayed behind in the visitors' center, doing nothing. Waiting. After forty-five minutes they should have been back. I was getting antsy and, after the incident with Audrey, a little nervous. I put up the AWAY sign and walked into the house. I heard them upstairs, *up* upstairs, in the Sky Parlor. I tiptoed up, hoping to hear the tour's final monologue, which would mean everything was fine and we could all go home soon.

From halfway up the stairs I heard James say, "Oh heck!" A pause. "No one's here. Just for you, for you the writer and reader, to encourage you to write because it's a hard job and an important job, because of that, we'll open the shades. Just for a minute. Just so you can see." My heart stopped. I could hear the plastic rolling upward. I didn't dare move.

"Beautiful," said the father.

"You see how he wrote at the desk? With his back to the window?" And then I heard it, the clink of metal, the sound of a hook coming out of its loop, a velvet rope being taken down.

"I'm not supposed to do this," he said, "but you've traveled a distance. Go ahead, stand in front of it."

My breathing was heavy. I tried to stay quiet. I thought I would cry.

"What's the matter?" I heard him say. For a moment I thought he was speaking to me, but he didn't even know I was there.

"Aren't you going to touch it?" I could hear his smile.

"Can I?"

Maybe he let one person touch it each summer, chose the person who would benefit most, who would receive the magic he believed was in it and then would use that magic. I could imagine her touching it, standing behind the unhooked rope, the light on her back, feeling like a writer with a world of possibilities open to her because she knew exactly what she wanted and everyone believed she would get it. I thought of Audrey and her journalism, the doors that had closed on her for reasons I couldn't understand. And I thought of myself, aimed at no door in particular, making decisions that now seemed random, standing on the steps of a home where three great writers had walked and kissed and talked and cried, and me there now, crying for the first time that summer.

★ ★ ★

"Are you sure you're all right?" James asked when we were both back in the visitors' center closing up.

"Uh-huh," was all I could muster.

"Are you thinking of Audrey?"

"Uh-huh," I said again, and I was. I was thinking of how much she wanted to be an adulteress like Hester Prynne, a heroic outcast, and how much she wanted to be a broadcast journalist, and how mean she was most of the time, and how messily she ate her pickles, which was probably why no one wanted her to broadcast the news. I thought of how she deserved to touch the desk more than I did and how I deserved it more than that woman who had traipsed through last minute like that. How my father thought James wanted me in the way that Audrey wanted someone, anyone. How James wasn't like that at all, but how I wished that he wanted me in some way, any way. How I had gotten what Audrey had wanted, but in the end maybe it wasn't even what she'd really wanted. Right then I wanted to live in the ugliness of the dying Wayside the way I sometimes thought I could sleep forever near the Old North Bridge. I wanted to make a home there, and I didn't know why.

"I think I'll be a writer," I said.

"It's a hard life. You have time. You can do anything," said James, smiling, dusting the shoulder of Nathaniel Hawthorne.

But he didn't believe me, and I never touched it.

ACKNOWLEDGMENTS

Thank you to everyone who made this book possible, including my agent, Jenni Ferrari-Adler, at Union Literary and my editor, Jean Garnett, at Little, Brown. Much gratitude also to Carina Guiterman for acquiring the book and Lauren Harms and Patrick Cullum for creating my dream cover. Thanks also to Sally Wofford-Girand, Karen Landry, Nell Beram, Jayne Yaffe Kemp, Abby Reilly, Reagan Arthur, Bruce Nichols, Jeffrey Gantz, and the entire team at Little, Brown.

I'm also grateful to the editors and staff at the literary magazines where many of these stories were first published, some in earlier or different forms: *Alaska Quarterly Review, Bare Fiction, Carolina Quarterly, Epoch, Indiana Review, Michigan Quarterly Review, Southeast Review,* and the *Threepenny Review.*

The University of Virginia MFA provided funding and time essential to an early writer, in addition to a talented crew of peers who read early versions of many of these stories and made them better: Colleen Hubbard, Greg Jackson, Kidda Johnson, Caitlin Kindervatter-Clark, Jenna Krumminga, Lulu Miller, Stephanie Milner, Alexis Schaitkin, Greg Seib, Dave Serafino, Joe Sills, and

Matthew Silva. Thanks also to those special teachers from grade school to grad school who challenged me, endured me, and let me imagine I could become a writer.

Finally, but not lastly, I'm lucky to have a vast and loving support system. I'm grateful to Derek Denman for helping me to turn my Fake Fake World into my Real Real World, for meeting me where I am and then pushing me forward; Amanda Barrett for her rare and generous friendship, for being the kind of friend who helps you pack and then falls asleep making pom-poms with you; Joe and Sarah Adelmann for their magic combo of tough love and loving support; my extended family—music-video performers and receivers of handmade gifts—who encouraged my creativity early and fell victim to it often; and my parents, Karin Hansen and Richard Adelmann, who raised me, taught me, and believed in me first.

AUTHOR'S NOTE

The title "None of These Will Bring Disaster" is borrowed from the Elizabeth Bishop poem "One Art." The story was inspired by Deborah Eisenberg's "Days," which can be found in *The Collected Stories of Deborah Eisenberg*. Stories from Lorrie Moore's collection *Self-Help* influenced the structure of "How to Wait" and "Elegy." Indeed, the first line of "Elegy" is a nod to the first line of "How to Talk to Your Mother," which also runs backward through time.

ABOUT THE AUTHOR

Maria Adelmann's work has been published by *Tin House*, *n+1*, the *Threepenny Review*, *Indiana Review*, *Epoch*, *McSweeney's Internet Tendency*, and other publications. She has received fellowships from Cornell University and the University of Virginia, where she earned her BA and MFA, respectively. Adelmann has had quite a few jobs (visual merchandiser, writing instructor, hotel reviewer) in quite a few cities (New York, Baltimore, Copenhagen) and once on a ship. She enjoys learning new crafts and letting personal projects take over her life. You can visit her online at mariaink.com or on Twitter and Instagram @ink176.